Pillow of Clouds

MARC TALBERT

AN AUTHORS GUILD BACKINPRINT.COM EDITION

AN AUTHORS GUILD BACKINPRINT.COM EDITION

Published by iUniverse.com, Inc.

For information address:
iUniverse.com, Inc.
620 North 48th Street, Suite 201
Lincoln, NE 68504-3467
www.iuniverse.com

Originally published by Dial Books for Young Readers

ISBN: 0-595-09770-7

Printed in the United States of America

*To Richard Peck, Lois Duncan,
Rosemary Wells, Will Hobbs
for their courage to write for children.*

M. T.

▼▼▼▼▼▼▼▼▼▼▼

PART I

There is a wall
Observed a cat
And over it she sprang

CHESTER HORNIG

ONE

▼▼▼▼▼▼▼▼▼▼▼

The intense afternoon sunlight made everything look
bleached—bleached and flat and somehow brittle, like
the color photos in the sort of magazine that you hide
from your parents outside the house. And I felt bleached
and flat and tired, yellowed around the edges and curled
at the corners. And crinkled, the way those kinds of
magazines get when they're handled too much by nervous, sweaty hands.

And my feet hurt. It was probably from the tire rut I
was walking in. My feet are wide and the rut was narrow. I looked down to see if my feet were folding
lengthwise in my sneakers, like the first step in making
a paper airplane. That's when my glasses slipped down
my nose for the millionth time that day. There's nothing more tiresome than constantly pushing up glasses.

So I let them sit where my nose flares into nostrils. Looking over them made me feel old and wise. And feeble. Sucking in my lips, I pretended not to have any teeth as I walked along in the rut, breathing through my mouth and taking the small, tottering steps of an old man. When the rut finally turned off into a driveway, I continued on my way, my feet spreading out, growing relaxed as a duck's.

With my glasses like that the only things I could see clearly were directly in front of my sneakers—mostly cement-hard dirt mixed with pebbles. But off to the side was a clump of wilted daylilies growing in front of a stone wall stretching along the other side of the irrigation ditch that followed the street.

I love that ditch. If I'd grown up in Santa Fe I would have made it into a private, make-believe river—my very own Nile or Amazon or Mississippi—for floating things down or for messing around in. The *acequia madre* it's called—the mother ditch—because it feeds all the smaller ditches that branch off it like the network of blood vessels on the back of my hand. Most days the *acequia madre* pulses with water, but today it was dry.

Everything was dry. I was dry. The air was dry. My thoughts were dry. Even the sunlight seemed powdery and dry. It settled on my shoulders and head with the softness of dust, accumulating in thick, warm layers before puffs of wind blew them off, leaving behind a naked sort of chilliness.

Mostly, though, my feelings were as dry and raw as the burned and peeling skin on my nose and chin. I'd been walking all day in the hot, baking August sun without a hat, trying to avoid the thing I hate most: saying good-bye—good-bye to Santa Fe, to José, to Florence, and to my father.

Saying good-bye tears me up inside. I sometimes stop reading books halfway through because by that point I'm already saying good-bye to the characters and missing them so much, I can't concentrate on the story. I've missed out on a lot of good books that way.

I've thought about it a lot, trying to figure out why I feel this way. I've come up with many possible reasons. But right now I figure that saying good-bye feels too much like practicing to die. Like most people, I don't think I'm ever *really* going to die or that the people I care about are ever *really* going to die. But that doesn't mean I don't think about it a lot, imagining all the different, gruesome ways it could happen.

Saying good-bye to Santa Fe was especially hard. I'd been visiting my father for the summer. Before I came, I wasn't looking forward to the visit. For one thing, I'd never been away from my mother for this long—almost three months. I knew I'd miss her—her sense of humor, her twinkling eyes, her way of mimicking other people's voices and faces and walks, her spooky way of knowing what I'm feeling or thinking even before I know myself. And I was worried—worried about her drinking and her depressions—worried about the days she didn't get out of bed or open the curtains in her bedroom—worried about the days when her words didn't come out right and tears came easily to her eyes.

For another thing, I'd never seen my father happy. Oh, I'd seen him loose-as-a-goose happy when he was

drinking with my mother. But after he stopped drinking, his face froze and his lips almost disappeared. I
didn't much want to spend a summer with a man with
big sad eyes who did nothing but read and write and
play moody classical music in his study.

As it turned out, I hardly recognized him when he
met me at the Albuquerque airport. It was like meeting
him for the first time. His eyes still had a hint of sadness about them, but it wasn't a bad kind of sadness.
It was a wise kind of sadness.

It was a shock to realize that for my father, getting
divorced from my mother and moving to Santa Fe and
opening a bookstore and living with Florence were
probably the best things that had ever happened to him.
An even bigger shock was finally realizing—after several weeks of not wanting to admit this—that coming
to visit my father was probably the best thing that had
ever happened to me. Seeing my father happy made me
realize how unhappy I'd been back in Iowa. It made
me realize how much I'd been like my father—how sad
and quiet.

I don't mean to give the impression that my mother
is a terrible person. She can be dazzling. But she's dazzling in a way that reminds me of one of those gor-
geous imported cars she sells along with the Chevies
at her dealership: Racing one would be great . . . if you
dared. My mother can take you on quite an emotional
ride when she wants to—exciting, scary, dangerous,
beautiful, fast. She can make life seem like fishtailing
down a winding country road at one hundred miles an
hour. With her you live for days with your heart in

your throat. But the crash always comes at the end of those crazy rides. Whoever is nearest to her—usually me or my dad—ends up battered and bruised. And out of the ruptured fuel tank comes the smell of Scotch instead of gasoline. To fight the pain of crashing she drinks. And to fight the loneliness of drinking she demands my time, until I sometimes have no time for myself.

The thing of it was, I didn't have to say good-bye to Santa Fe. Knowing this rubbed hot spots in my mind, like the hot spots on the soles and heels of my feet from walking around town. Even though I was scheduled to fly into Des Moines tomorrow, I didn't have to go. I could decide to stay in Santa Fe and go to school here. It was my choice—to stay or to go back to Iowa. You see, both my parents wanted me to live with them after their divorce. And in typical fashion the two of them weren't grown-up enough to make that decision.

Looking back, I can't remember that they agreed on anything. Just as an example, when I finally understood how babies are made, I was amazed, wondering how my parents could ever have agreed to do that—that thing. I couldn't imagine them ever making love. I still can't.

It made me wonder for a long time about whether I might be adopted. But then I couldn't imagine their agreeing on what kind of kid they would want to adopt any more than I could imagine them making love. In some strange way it made me feel that maybe I'd found them, picked them, had them—instead of the other way around.

Anyway, when the divorce got really nasty, their clever lawyers came up with a clever compromise. It must have pleased them, because they signed on the dotted lines without first consulting me. If they had asked, I would have told them what a horrible thing it was they wanted me to do. I would have told them how impossible it was, how cruel. According to the papers they signed, I was supposed to choose which parent to live with when I turned thirteen. In other words I was supposed to choose one parent and reject the other one. Either way I couldn't win. Either way, I would hurt one of them.

Well, I'd turned thirteen while I was in Santa Fe. It was time.

I thought I knew what I was supposed to do. I didn't want to go back, but I felt that it was my duty. I figured that my father had Florence and that my mother . . . well, I figured that my mother had me.

So, as part of saying good-bye, I was pretending to gather images and impressions of Santa Fe for a poem I wanted to write, a poem to commemorate my summer. I wanted to distill Santa Fe in a few perfect words, each word's meaning and energy linked to every other word's meaning and energy.

Anyway, I was running out of steam, circling around and around the old area of town where my father and Florence live. The dirt street I was walking on wound through a shallow, narrow valley that was clogged with houses and shops and art galleries. I was pretty much alone, because the sun can beat down hard enough at this time of day to give you a headache. I felt as if I'd been clobbered. And by then I wasn't even pretending to gather material for my poem. With my glasses practically perched on my upper lip, I couldn't see much of anything anyway. Instead I was concentrating on the feel of the untucked tail of my shirt flapping whenever a puff of air hit it just right.

I looked up, throwing my head back so that I could see through my glasses. Just as I expected, I found myself in front of my father's house. I veered off the dirt road and walked up the short driveway that ends in a carport. Florence's car sat underneath, and with my glasses teetering on the tip of my nose, I noticed that its tires were a little flat because it hadn't been driven for a month or more. Around the carport is a trail that climbs the hill behind my father's house. Every time I scramble up that trail, the hill's shape reminds me of a giant bald head, a head as ugly as I imagine my own would be without hair. And the trail reminds me of a part line—a groove dug into the hill's scalp after years of dragging a comb through hair that has long since disappeared.

I pushed my glasses to the top of my nose, took a deep breath, and trudged up the trail. My feet felt heavy and I was tired. When I came out of the hill's shade and into the sunlight, I let my legs fold under me, turning as if I were corkscrewing into the ground. Looking around, I noticed I'd barely missed sitting on a barrel cactus that was no bigger than a quarter.

After all that walking around town it felt good to sit. It felt especially good to sit on the top of this hill, overlooking Santa Fe. During the summer it was the place

I often came to, to sit among the scrubby buffalo grasses and the short, stunted bushes with tiny gray leaves that turned pale green in the light of the setting sun. This was my place to be alone, to write poems.

The trouble was, I hadn't written any poems so far that summer. Poems come easiest to me when I'm drawn into myself and sad. Back home, in Iowa, I wrote poetry almost every day. I had notebooks full of the stuff, hidden with some "special" magazines in a metal box under some bushes in the backyard. The first week I was in Santa Fe, before I met José, I'd come up to the top of the hill every day with some paper and a pencil nub stuffed into my back pocket. I'd sit for hours, looking at the city below me, waiting for poetry to fall from the sky and hit me like a piece of a fractured satellite. Before too long I forgot all about poetry. Instead I'd stare, fascinated, at the twinkles and gleams of car windshields through the droopy leaves of the trees. I'd marvel at the houses that looked more like sand castles than anything else. The adobe walls of these houses were dented and bent with the shadows of trees, and they had soft and rounded corners and flat roofs covered with gray gravel. And scattered through the city were the most incredible hills—hills the color of tanned flesh and so steep they reminded me of bent bare knees pointing skyward. Or breasts.

After a while I didn't even bother to bring paper and a pencil up to the top of this hill. I felt as if I were living a poem, not writing one. In fact, all summer I felt as if I were the main character of a wonderful book, a character that was as interested as the reader in what was going to happen next. I didn't want to say good-bye to the character I had become, and surprisingly, I didn't want to put the book down partway through.

Sometimes I just sat for hours and stared at the blue sky. But today, as I stared, the sky was not quite flawless.

A single small cloud was floating slowly from west to east, and perhaps a little bit north. It wasn't much of a cloud—being raggedy, the color of dustballs, and no particular shape. But it was the only cloud in the sky, which made it seem important.

By then my glasses were slipping downward again and I scrunched my nose several times in an effort to push them up to where they belonged. They stayed where they were and I left them alone. Leaning back on my elbows, I sighted between the rough-skinned knobbiness of my drawn-up knees, pretending they were new hills thrust up in the middle of Santa Fe. I tilted my head back so that I could squint through my glasses at the cloud. Never before had I given a cloud my undivided attention, and the idea of doing this intrigued me. So I sat on top of the hill and struggled to concentrate on that cloud, to keep my mind from wandering and drifting.

It was hard work. Even though I kept my eyes fixed on the cloud, my thoughts raced around it, moving like a silent sheepdog herding a lone lamb toward a flock that was somewhere out of sight—maybe behind the mountains to the west or the east, maybe below the horizon to the south. When I caught my thoughts doing this, I'd jerk them back, making them heel.

I remember that the sun shone down with a brightness that almost hummed. Maybe that humming was the beginning of a headache, caused by being in the sun so much as I walked all over town.

As I watched, the cloud slowly grew, its leading edge flattening as if it had bumped against something solid. I held my breath as the cloud began to pull in on itself, to shrink, to pause, seeming almost to move backward, against the wind. And then, as the cloud resumed its eastward journey, it came closer to the sun and began to fade, as if the sun were boiling it dry.

At that point it was too close to the sun to watch without hurting my eyes. So I sat up, hugging my knees to my chest, and leaned forward to see my father's house better. At the beginning of the summer I'd never seen another house like it. From where I sat I saw its flat, graveled roof. Asters grew where dirt and leaves gathered behind the western parapet wall, protected from the wind. From the first time I noticed them, I liked the idea of flowers taking root on the roof. They grew above the room I slept in, the spare room with its piles of books and the couch that pulled out into a bed.

My father told me that the house was old, maybe close to one hundred years old. It seemed to grow out of the earth. The plaster covering the adobe mud walls was cracked, especially at the corners and around the turquoise-blue windows. Some of the plaster was flaking off in patches that showed the chicken wire underneath.

For a moment, looking at my father's house, I felt horrible about going back to Iowa the next day. But my mind was made up and I couldn't allow myself to feel that way, so I quickly looked up, beyond my father's house, out over the city. My glasses crept even farther down my nose and I tried to ignore them, looking over their tops. Santa Fe was blurry, its colors and shapes mushed together. It was startling how much Santa Fe now looked much as I imagined Clifton, my hometown in Iowa, would look to a flying bird. The hills and sky blended along the horizon, reminding me of the heavy dirt-blown Iowa sky in late summer, just before harvest. Even though I thought I knew Santa Fe well, I couldn't distinguish between the houses and the dirt from which they got their color. The trees were a blanket of green and could have been a stretch of Carr's Park back home. And the main highway that cut through Santa Fe going north could have been the Skunk River.

All my life people have pointed out the differences between places. But right now, without my glasses, Santa Fe and Clifton appeared almost the same. It was a wonderful thought. For the first time a voice inside of me said, "Santa Fe could be home!" But as soon as my mind gave voice to that thought, I stiffened. It seemed a dangerous and selfish and wicked thing to think.

Angry with myself, I pushed up my glasses with a trembling middle finger and Santa Fe came back into focus, all of its differences crisp and clear. It was hard to believe that the city below me had reminded me of Clifton just moments before.

And then I remembered the cloud I'd been studying earlier. I leaned back onto my elbows again and scanned the painfully blue desert above me, once more amazed by its color—a blue so deep and pure that it didn't seem quite real.

Just as I'd decided the cloud was gone, I noticed a smudge in the sky, off to one side. I squinted and watched the smudge grow clearer, taking on a pale color, blossoming white. Slowly, it took on a shape—a shape like a crab walking sideways across the sky. Tendrils of cloud stuck out from the main body, moving slowly and stiffly. As I watched, the legs pulled in and the cloud grew, slowly unfolding.

Mesmerized, I kept my eyes on that little cloud, watching it grow, feeling very lucky that I'd witnessed its birth—or rebirth. The hill was becoming uncomfortable, sharp little rocks digging into my elbows and forearms. And as the cloud grew larger it also seemed to become more comfortable—like a pillow.

Pillow of clouds. I closed my eyes, letting that phrase ring in my head. It was a lovely thought—the first poetic thought I'd had all summer. If I'd had paper and a pencil, I'd have written it down. It was the seed of a poem, a tiny seed, and I was afraid to lose it before it could take root and grow in my head, afraid to let other weedy thoughts strangle it.

Opening my eyes I saw that the cloud was now stretched thin. As it glided across the sky, it shrank and grew, as if breathing deeply, slowly. It seemed to speed up as it approached the mountains in the east, the Sangre de Cristos.

And then, too soon, it disappeared in a slot between two peaks.

TWO

▼▼▼▼▼▼▼▼▼▼▼

"Chester! Chester!"

I heard my name called over and over, becoming more breathless and faint even as the sounds of scrambling and rocks crunched against rocks grew louder. I tried to keep from smiling, but the corners of my mouth twitched with happiness as I turned toward the hill's front and the head of the trail. I almost called a greeting but decided not to. Instead I watched silently as a mop of black hair appeared over the crest of the hill. Next came the round face of my friend José. When he saw me, his face split into a smile that was as bright as a quarter moon and almost exactly the same shape, rocking up on one side.

"Ai-eee!" José exclaimed, throwing himself onto the

ground next to me, barely missing the barrel cactus himself. I could feel the heat being thrown off by his body and I could smell his sweat, which had aged during the day to the odor of weak vinegar. José gasped for a minute or two, his chest heaving, his shirt pulling apart in front between the straining buttons. He looked at me, still struggling to control his breathing. "I . . . I looked all over for you . . . up and down the . . . the arroyo and even . . . even in your papa's store . . . among all the books and everything. I should have known I'd find you here."

I nodded and smiled, remembering the first time we'd met. It was on this hill, where we were now sitting. I'd been daydreaming, lost in thought. And then suddenly there was this kid standing in front of me. He was studying me from a safe distance, like I was some kind of strange cactus that could launch barbs at him.

"What are you doing here?" he'd asked, in English seasoned with Spanish.

"Sitting," I'd replied. And then, as if that wasn't enough reason to be where I was, I'd added, "Thinking."

"Oh." He sounded somehow disappointed. Without bothering to ask if I minded, he'd sat down beside me. Peeved, I almost got up and left, but I felt that he was the one who should leave. After all, I'd wanted to be alone and I'd been there first.

He didn't seem to mind my rude silence. And slowly, without even noticing, I relaxed and accepted his presence—his breathing, his chucking small rocks down the hill, his humming beneath his breath. We sat there for the rest of the afternoon—mostly thinking, sometimes talking, growing comfortable and friendly with each other.

That afternoon, on top of this hill, I made the best friend I've ever had. In some ways I was dreading saying good-bye to José more than saying good-bye to my father and Florence. I'd avoided him all day, but deep inside I must have known that he'd track me down. At least I wanted him to.

Now José leaned back on an elbow and straightened his entire body as he reached into the pocket of his jeans, pulling out a little sack of piñon nuts. "Want some?" he asked, unrolling the top of the sack and pinching the paper into a spout. He shook a small pile into the palm of his other hand, pellets of tarnished bronze the size of soybeans back home.

I almost shook my head no and then changed my mind. "Sure." I took a couple from José's palm and watched as he popped the two remaining nuts into his mouth. He worked his jaw almost imperceptibly and then spit out the thin-skinned hulls: four neat, empty halves. José had spent much of the summer trying to teach me to crack and shell the little nuts in my mouth, using only my tongue and teeth. I was getting better at it, but even so, most of the time I ended up chewing some of the shell along with the rich, sweet meat.

I was a bit nervous as I stuck a piñon nut into my mouth and tried to maneuver it around so that it sat in the crown of a molar. It didn't help to see José staring at me, moving his jaw, shadowing each move I was making. I moved my jaw a little to the side and then brought my teeth together slowly, tensing, ready to ease up the exact moment I felt the shell give and begin to split. José's large brown eyes made me nervous, maybe because they looked so hopeful that this time I'd get it right. Slowly, slowly I brought my jaws together, and before I could stop myself, I heard a noise like a tree falling and my teeth crushed the piñon nut—shell and all.

"*Pla-a-th!*" I said, making a face and spitting out the debris. "I'll never get it."

"Sure you will," José said, generously. "You just need to practice more. I'll give you some for the airplane and you can practice all the way back to Iowa. Practice hard, so that when you come back you can eat piñones in the classroom so skillfully that your teachers won't even know when they look you right in your ugly freckled face."

I grunted. José was certain that I'd be coming back next week to start school. José's certainty was unnerving. I'd explained it several times and still he didn't seem to understand how serious the problem was, how impossible it would be to tell my mother that I wanted to live with my father.

I didn't want to say anything, so I popped another nut into my mouth and moved it around with my tongue. It felt huge—the size of a marble at least. José burst out laughing and I looked up at him, wondering what I'd done wrong.

He shrugged his shoulders and lifted his eyebrows in a mock apology. "Amigo, you look like you have a *cucaracha* in your mouth," he said. And then he imitated me—his mouth scrunching up, his eyebrows colliding, his tongue stretching his cheeks out as it groped around in his mouth, his lips pressed tightly, moving up and down and sideways.

I couldn't help myself: I grinned. It was funny. José often made fun of me in a gentle way that wasn't mean, that made me laugh at myself. I'd find myself puffing up in anger and then realize how ridiculous I must look. I'd laughed at myself more this summer than I had in my entire life.

But, in grinning, my tongue relaxed and the piñon nut slipped over the back of my tongue. I gagged and swallowed at the same time.

"Ugh!" I sputtered. "I swallowed the whole thing!" I felt a little bead of hardness creeping down my throat. And then my stomach tightened, as if I'd swallowed a golf ball instead of a tiny piñon nut.

"Don't worry," José said, rolling the top of the bag over onto itself. "My grandmother always says that they come out as easy as they go in." He straightened out again, slipping the bag back into his pocket. "Hey! I almost forgot." He sat up and his eyes twinkled. "Arturo got the engine going on the Red Devil and says that we can go for a ride."

"Really?" I'd wanted to ride in the Red Devil all summer, but José's older brother had never gotten the engine of his '57 Chevy to work. He kept finding things wrong with it and spent most of his time looking for parts in junkyards as far away as Albuquerque and Española and Taos. When he got the engine working right, Arturo was going to make a low-rider out of it—a car of chrome and metallic paint and thick fake fur on the dash and quilted upholstery and a hydraulic suspension that allowed its rear end to buck like a rodeo bronco and that allowed the whole car to drag on the ground, shooting sparks where its metal scraped the pavement.

"Yeah," José said. "We should hurry before the engine discovers it's been tricked." He scrambled to his feet and I was only a moment behind him.

My feet slipped and slid as I trotted down the twisty back of the hill, plunging into the cool shadow of the valley and the sounds of birds chirping and the smells of flowers. José, whose legs and arms weren't stretched too long and thin from fast growing, was more nimble. He avoided the larger rocks that turned my ankles and made me wave my arms around for balance. My glasses almost fell off, forcing me to grab hold of them with one hand and wave for balance with the other. I was glad he was ahead of me and couldn't see how stupid I must have looked—like an ostrich trying to fly . . . or dance.

I sighed with relief at the bottom of the hill. We trotted around the carport to the dirt street and turned left, passing in front of my father's house. Everything was dirt and dust and brightness on the street side of the adobe walls we passed. One wall sloped downward into rubble, and where it left off another wall reared straight up. This wall had several irregular-shaped openings at different levels—*nichos* and whimsical windows. The wall we passed curved and undulated, shrinking and growing in a playful manner.

My summer had been like that—whimsical and playful, meandering and irregular and soft. In Iowa, with the harsh heat and humidity, where the air itself feels sweaty, I'd always carried myself prickly as barbed wire, stretching between spring and fall by the shortest, quickest, most no-nonsense route.

Through gaps in the walls for driveways or walkways, I glimpsed the lushness of people's yards—velvet lawns bordered with crazy-quilt collections of flowers that attracted hummingbirds and butterflies. And cats, of course.

José darted across the street and I was close behind, taking one step for every two of his. Before I could stop myself, I ducked my head as we went through a wide arched gate, instantly feeling silly because the gate was easily tall enough for a big man to go under. The dark, thick shadow it cast made the archway seem lower than it was, and the illusion tricked me every time.

The rutted driveway bent to the right and around a low adobe house that was mostly hidden behind large bushes and trees. The Chevy was parked under a wide carport at the end of the driveway. The car faced out, its hood yawning and its dull headlights staring in a tired and bored way. The grille smirked at us in that pinched way of old cars, toothy and smug as a ten-year-old with new shoes.

A lean figure was draped over the front fender, its head lost inside the engine's cavity. Arturo was reaching into the engine so deeply that his feet weren't touching the ground and his T-shirt rode up his back, exposing ribs almost to his armpits. A grunt came from the car, loud and sudden, as if the engine had burped in Arturo's face.

Seeing Arturo this way made me smile. Even though José had brought me out to the carport several times during my first few weeks in Santa Fe, I'd never really gotten a good look at Arturo's face. I would have recognized Arturo's rear end anyplace—sticking up and plumping half out of his jeans as he bent into the engine of his car. And I would have recognized his feet as they stuck out from underneath the car's bumper lip. But I wouldn't have recognized Arturo's face until halfway through the summer when he'd suddenly looked up from his work, grease smudged around his neck and eyes where he'd scratched himself or wiped away sweat. He'd told José to fetch him a Coke, all the time looking at me. And then, without another word, he'd dived back into his car's engine.

"Arturo!" José sauntered up to his brother and peered into the engine. "Why isn't the Red Devil running? This car acting like your girlfriend again?"

Arturo's shoulders remained where they were. But he slowly lifted his head, his eyes showing white underneath as they aimed bad thoughts past his forehead. "Do I hear the sound of a mosquito sucking a drunk man's blood?" he asked, glowering at José.

José laughed out loud. "E-e-e-e! That was a good one, bro!"

I stood off to the side, grinning stupidly. I love listening to José and Arturo throw insults back and forth. I'm never quick enough to come up with such wisecracks myself.

Arturo tightened his mouth to keep from smiling. "Why did the chicken cross the road?" he asked slowly, speaking to José but glancing at me to make sure I was paying attention too.

José sidled over to Arturo and leaned against a fender. Having José so close to his brother made me nervous. I was bursting to tell him that he was walking into a trap. José didn't seem to understand and he narrowed his eyes, stroked his pointy chin, and thought for a moment. "I don't know. Why?"

"To get away from his older brother!" Arturo yelled, dropping to his feet and lunging for José.

"Help!" José cried, turning too late.

"Cheek-on-n-n!" Arturo yelled, grabbing José from behind in a bear hug, pinning his arms to his sides, and lifting him off the ground. Arturo squeezed hard and both he and José grunted at the same time. I was caught between wanting to help José and wanting to run. A nervous giggle escaped from my open mouth, and I felt myself turning a deeper red than my sunburn.

Arturo let go of José, and before turning back to his car he rumpled his younger brother's head. "You're more trouble than green chili for breakfast," he said in his low, almost lazy, voice.

"And *you* look like sugar but you taste like salt," José chanted, putting the car between himself and his older brother. I walked around the car to be next to José. I wanted to share in the fun, but at the same time I was afraid of the roughhousing these two brothers did all the time. José leaned over the car and almost crowed.

"Maybe that's why girls don't like you for long." I could tell that José thought his comment was very funny by the way he struggled to keep from laughing as he spoke.

Arturo stared at us and tried to look angry. When he saw that we were ready to push off from the car and run away, he laughed instead. "What would you know about girls, anyway," he said in a teasing voice. "Salt brings out the flavor of things and sugar is just empty calories. If you ask me, you look like *salt* and taste like *sugar*, baby bro. You'd better look for a girl that likes junk food, 'cause that's what you are!"

José playfully stuck his elbow into my side and winked at me. And then, rolling his eyes, he tipped his head toward his brother. Abruptly he stopped his pantomine and leaned over the engine. "What happened, anyway? It was working an hour ago."

Arturo's smile melted and he gazed down at his engine, chewing on his lower lip. "I don't know. It was purring like a *gato* and then it got the hiccups and then it stopped. I don't know. Maybe bad gas. Maybe a loose hose. Maybe . . ." He leaned closer and peered into a cranny I couldn't see. "E-ho-lay. Well, I'll be . . ."

We watched as Arturo's head and shoulders disappeared on the other side of the engine. We heard banging, followed by muttering. I felt another elbow in my ribs and looked over at José. He was pointing to the open door on the driver's side. Taking exaggerated sneaking steps I followed him around the back of the car. We eased the back of the driver's seat forward and crawled behind it, careful that we didn't jiggle the car or cause the suspension to groan, even though the suspension was probably rusted solid like the rest of the car.

"Bounce on the count of three," José whispered, cranking up his elbows like wings, his fisted hands down toward his belly, his legs tense and ready. "One . . . two . . . three!"

We both pushed off from the floor and began to bounce up and down on the backseat of the Chevy, making it hop stiffly like a slow-cruising low-rider.

"Hey!" Arturo sounded surprised.

"Quick. Out the other door!" José dived over the front seat and pulled the driver's door closed. He shoved down the lock just as his brother's grimy, angry face appeared at the grimier window. By this time I was launched over the front seat, but my legs were tangled around each other. With a grunt I pulled them apart and rammed the passenger door open with my shoulder. My heart was beating in my ears and I half fell, half scrambled out the door. José was close behind.

Arturo was rushing around the back of the car, fire in his eyes. "You lousy kids! I almost had it and then you made the screwdriver screw up!" He was puffing with frustration and I was honestly scared of the screwdriver he held in his hand.

We left the door open, which luckily slowed Arturo down, and rushed around to the opposite side of the car. "Hey! Cool your jets, bro." I was not reassured to see that José's eyes were big with fear. "It was a joke. We didn't mean nothing, man!"

Arturo slammed the passenger door shut and scrambled after us. To make us move faster, we pushed off the car with our hands, bouncing around it three times. Once, Arturo pretended to double back and almost tricked us into running right into him. Nobody said anything, but the carport was filled with the sound of heavy breathing and feet shuffling and stuttering on the dirt, loud as a basketball game.

Finally, when we were in front of the car, at the mouth of the carport, José shouted, "Run for it!" We sprinted down the driveway as if a bear were chasing us. Holding on to my glasses with one hand and punching air with my other, I ran faster than I ever had in my life, spurred on by imagining that José's panting was really Arturo breathing down our necks.

Just when I was about to collapse, I noticed that José was no longer next to me. I skidded to a stop and turned around. José had stopped a few yards back, his hands on his knees and his arms propping up his shoulders. Arturo leaned on the Chevy and polished one set of fingernails on the front of his shirt. He hadn't even tried to follow us.

"Ee-ho-lay!" José gasped, turning around to check on me. He gulped some more air and turned back to his brother.

"We got you good!" he called.

I didn't trust Arturo's smile or the way he looked relaxed. "Come on," I whispered. "Let's get out of here."

"He can't catch us," José whispered back over his shoulder, keeping an eye on his brother. "He smokes too much."

"Don't worry, little *pescado*," said Arturo in a voice

that almost sounded bored. "I'll get you back. Maybe tonight when you're asleep." He glanced down at his fingernails and smiled down at them. When he raised his head he looked at me. "Hey, Chester." I stared back, wondering what was going to happen next. "Have a safe trip to Ohio or Idaho or wherever you're going."

"I-oh-wah!" I shouted before I could stop myself.

"Whatever." Arturo laughed as he turned back to his car. He'd gotten me—good.

"Who-ee! That was close," José said as we walked around the house, toward the street. "I think he was really mad for a second or two."

"Will he really get you?" I asked. I was sweating like crazy. This was not running weather.

"Naw. He'll forget. The only thing he ever remembers are the number of buttons on the backs of his girl-friends' dresses."

We turned right, onto the street, and headed back to my house. Midstep, I panicked. It was time. This was my time to say good-bye to José.

José must have felt the same, because the silence between us was now awkward, begging to be broken. I stole a glance at José and saw that he was concentrating on the ground in front of his feet.

"Hey, José?" My voice was like a little kid's and I quickly cleared my throat.

He looked up, his eyes hopeful and sad at the same time.

"I guess . . . I mean . . ." I didn't know what to say.

"Look," José said, frowning. "I don't know nothing

28

▼

about Iowa. I don't know nothing about your mother. But I *do* know I don't want you to go."

I closed my mouth. I was hoping that José would be better at saying good-bye than I was, that he would help me, that he would make it easier. Instead he was making it harder. I stopped walking and jammed my hands into my pockets. I stared at José's feet, not wanting to look him in the eyes.

José stopped and faced me. "You told me you have to go back," he said. "I don't believe you."

Now, *that* startled me. I looked up so fast, my glasses almost flipped off. "What do you mean you don't believe me?" I was caught between anger and sorrow. "I *have* to go back. My mother *needs* me."

José shook his head impatiently, as if he were trying to shoo a circling fly. "Your father doesn't need you?" He jammed his hands into his pockets, just as I had, and looked down as he scuffed dirt with the toe of his sneaker. "Chester," he said, looking up, "do you like living here? In Santa Fe?"

I thought for a moment, wondering if I should be honest with him. "Yes." I didn't sound as sure as I felt.

"Are you happy back in Ohio?"

I began to protest, to say it was "Iowa," to spell it out in a patient but injured voice. When I saw his half grin and the twinkle in his eyes, I snorted softly.

His smile disappeared. "Well, are you? Happy, I mean . . . back there?"

I fought the word that finally came out of my mouth. "No."

"You could visit your mother. She could visit you. You could live here. If it didn't work out, you could move back to—"

"Iowa," we both said at the same time. Both of our smiles were tight and unsure.

"Yeah, that place," José said, "where the corn grows as tall as an elephant's lips and all of that." He cocked his head to one side. "There aren't elephants in Iowa, are there?"

"No." José was a nut. I was going to miss him. Terribly.

"Then why do they say that, about corn and elephants?"

I shrugged.

"Hey, I almost forgot." He dropped his shoulder as he rooted around in one of his pockets. He pulled out the bag of piñon nuts and thrust it toward me. "Here. For practicing."

I took the piñones from José. "Thanks," I managed to say.

The seconds of silence that followed seemed like minutes. "I guess I'd better get back home," José finally said. "My grandmother, she likes me to read the newspaper to her." His smile was rueful. "The obituaries, mostly. And her horoscope, even though the priest says it's a sin."

I opened my mouth. This was the time, and I wanted to get it over with.

"Don't say it," José interrupted.

I was relieved. "Okay. I won't say . . ."

"Good-bye!" José took a step toward me and punched

me on the shoulder. I'm sure he meant it to be playful, but it hurt like crazy. And his face looked strange, as if he were fighting a sneeze.

Before I could even reach up to rub my shoulder where he'd hit it, José spun around and raced down the road to his house. My mouth open and my chest hurting as much as my shoulder, I watched my friend turn and disappear through the archway of his family's driveway.

"Good-bye," I croaked to the empty street.

THREE

▼▼▼▼▼▼▼▼▼▼▼▼

I stood in the street for a moment, stunned, not knowing quite how I felt but knowing that I didn't like it. If
I were watching a movie, I'd have closed my eyes and
covered my ears at the part when José looked as if he
were going to burst into tears.

My nose began to drip—those cheating kind of tears
that don't come out properly—and I wiped it with the
back of the hand that was holding the bag of piñones.
I stuffed the bag into the pocket of my jeans and turned
back toward my father's house, my chest tight and my
eyes tingly. José hadn't even let me say good-bye and
I felt at loose ends and somehow to blame, as if I hadn't
done the job properly.

The closer I got to my father's house, the slower I
walked. I'd botched saying good-bye to José and now

I cringed, imagining the mess I was going to make of saying good-bye to my father and Florence.

So much for fading into the sunset.

As I turned into my father's driveway, I stopped and narrowed my eyes in concentration. I thought I had heard screaming. Now I heard nothing but the wind fluffing the leaves in the trees. And then I heard it again, clearly this time: screaming and hooting that sounded like gusts of pain and anger mixed together with shrieks of surprise. Oh, no, I thought, so loudly passersby might have heard. They're fighting. I'd never heard my father and Florence fight before, and this was proof of my feeling that it was too good to be true.

Hesitating, I tried to decide if I should wait out here until the fight was over or walk quietly into the house, sneak to my room, and start packing for tomorrow's trip. And then I heard laughter, shrill and breathless, followed by my father's guffaw.

It was a huge relief to hear that guffaw. I sprinted toward the house, threw open the front door, and almost collided with my father, who was leaping off an overstuffed chair, his arms waving in front of him, his mouth open wide, grimacing and smiling at the same time. Taking a half step backward, I saw a red-faced Florence across the room, standing on the sofa. She was stepping back and forth and back and forth to keep her balance on its lumpy, tipsy mushiness. She was frantically waving a newspaper in front of an open window, as if she were trying to empty the room of air. With each step her funny-shaped bare toes gripped the sofa's fabric before letting go.

33
▼

Suddenly I heard a whine and dipped my head just as a hummingbird zipped by—a blur of sound that stopped just before it hit the opposite wall. It hovered in the air, its wings invisible, the sound shrunk small. The tiny bird twitched back and forth, floating up and down as if on little waves, the cap of green feathers on its head dark inside the house. Its red throat pulsed, as if in fear, and my father stalked in front of me, trying to slip in around the back of the bird.

"Maybe we should leave it alone," Florence said breathlessly, in that voice of hers that always sounds like an operatic soprano singing and talking at the same time. "Maybe it'll go out the window on its own." She'd stopped waving the newspaper, but kept moving her feet for balance.

My father continued to maneuver around the bird. "I'm afraid it'll bang into something and do some damage to itself," he said. Pondering this a moment, I couldn't decide if he was agreeing or disagreeing with Florence.

Suddenly the bird pivoted toward me and bolted toward the daylight coming through the open door at my back. It looked as if it was aimed right between my eyes as it flashed toward me, sounding like a blender on high. "Ee-ack!" I squeaked, throwing my hands up against my face and closing my eyes. And then I heard a soft thump, and the bird's shrill humming stopped.

"Oh, dear," I heard Florence say. I opened my eyes, and through a maze of fingers I saw her hop off the couch and land heavily on a large Indian rug. I followed her gaze, turning toward the front door, and looked down.

The hummingbird lay on its back on the floor next to the doorjamb, its head tipped sideways, its eyes closed, a long delicate tongue hanging out the side of its partly opened beak.

"O-o-o-oh." The sound leaked from my mouth. I felt my father's hand on my shoulder as Florence dropped to her knees and gently swept the bird into the cupped palm of her hand. She grunted as she got to her feet and rested her hand atop the shelf of her bosom.

The bird was so small in her hand, its needle-thin beak almost as long as the rest of its body. In the light coming from the doorway its feathers shimmered, a rainbow of colors wicked out to the edge of each dark gray feather.

"I—I didn't mean to!" I blurted. The bird's shape blurred into a colorful puddle as my eyes filled with tears.

My father's hand tightened its grip on my shoulder. "It wasn't your fault."

I blinked away the blurriness of tears and sniffed, staring at the little bird in Florence's hand. I thought I saw its head twitch slightly, but decided that either tears were playing tricks with my eyes or the bird's muscles were giving up the last of their life's energy.

"My hands feel empty." Florence's usually robust voice was husky and quiet. "I don't believe I've ever seen anything so precious in my life."

I looked at Florence's face. It wasn't a pretty face,

but it looked comfortable and exactly right on her—a nice loose, honest fit. It was fleshy and, up close, covered with a network of very fine wrinkles. Up close she looked perhaps a little older than her forty years. But from a couple of feet away her wrinkles were too small to see, making her skin appear remarkably soft and young.

Florence looked over to me. "It came through the open window, came in after those ratty old geraniums that finally decided to bloom . . . you know, the ones by my easel." Her eyes were clear—unafraid and gentle and calm—and now sad. I nodded. "We chased it in here."

"Let's take it outside and look at it in a better light," my father suggested. "Most things don't look half as pretty alive as this little bird looks dead."

That was such a typical thing for my father to say—bookish and dreamy. For a moment I felt like telling my father that he should be writing books, not selling them. My insides were already wadded up from missing my father and I hadn't even packed yet.

"You're so right, Harvey." Florence could make my father's homely name quite beautiful. Mine too, for that matter.

My father and I stood back as Florence walked past us and through the front door. Her hands were held together in front of her, her head bowed as she looked at the bird. She walked slowly and smoothly, gliding, as if she were leading a procession at church. My father and I followed.

We stepped into a patch of light and Florence turned

around, straightening her arms to present the hummingbird to us. The bird's feathers caught the light and burst into a brilliance of color. I stepped closer, dazzled by what I saw.

And then suddenly, without warning, the bird exploded from Florence's hands.

"E-e-e-ouch!" Florence gasped, flapping her hands as if they'd been burned. "Holy cow!"

My father grunted and took a step back. "Well, I'll be . . ."

I was too startled to move.

A second too late we all looked to where the angry buzz of the hummingbird was disappearing. The sound seemed to linger behind like the exhaust of a jet, and the bird was now out of sight.

Florence's hands caught each other and held tight. She beamed at my father and me. "It must have just been in shock."

"Catatonic," my father said in his dreamy, thoughtful voice. "I've heard that their metabolism shuts down to almost nothing when they're in shock . . . or when they're sleeping."

I still couldn't believe what had happened, and my face must have shown the confusion of shock and relief that I felt. Florence stepped forward and took me into her arms. "Amazing," she said, stroking the back of my head. "But I bet it has a monstrous headache!"

My mother and father were never much for touching, except in anger. It took me a while to remember to reach around Florence and hug her back. She was big and my hands barely touched.

37
▼

"There, now," Florence said, letting go. "We'd better get dinner on the table. We don't want to send you back to Iowa with your bones sticking out."

I stepped back from Florence and looked at her shyly, struck by the wonder of her, by the ways in which she shared in my sadness as well as my happiness. She wasn't shy of helping herself to either, or any other emotion that I served up from time to time. It seemed that she enjoyed emotions in the same way she enjoyed food.

And then I noticed my father, standing off to the side, looking as if he wanted to say something but not knowing how to say it. When he saw me looking at him, he opened his mouth slightly, worked his tongue for a moment, and then said, "I'll bet you're hungry." He shut his mouth with a snap and swallowed, embarrassed that he hadn't been able to bring himself to say whatever he'd been feeling.

Florence put her arm around his shoulders and squeezed. "I think we might even have something for dinner that Chester actually likes."

"Chili chicken?" I asked.

She nodded, her smile smug. "You're going to miss green chili back in Iowa. Maybe even more than you miss your dad and me."

I was going to protest but caught myself in time. Instead, I smiled at her, realizing that she knew this wasn't true and that I knew it wasn't true. As I looked at her, I found myself longing to stay. This feeling almost took my breath away and I fought it, my mouth jerking into a frown. Florence studied me, trying to decipher the feelings I was trying to hide from her.

And then she smiled. "Come on, come on," she sang, herding my father and me into the house, toward the kitchen.

I loved this kitchen from the first time I saw it. It was a kitchen of loud colors and smells, of teetering stacks of pots and pans, of braided garlic and chili *ristras* and bunches of dried dill and a branch of bay leaves hanging from the ceiling. All the cupboards were open, with no doors, and were filled with food and plates and cups and warped Mexican glasses made from melted-down Coke bottles. The walls and countertops were covered with a patchwork of tiles from Mexico, their pattern a blue trellis on a cream background. Some of the tiles were almost as humped as starfish and others had corners that curled up like dry leaves. Nothing sat properly on them without first being shifted around to find the right combination of humps and dips.

"Would you set the table?" my father asked me.

"Sure." I walked to the cupboard and grabbed a stack of plates. I looped a finger of my other hand through the handles of three mugs and lifted them off the shelf. The mugs clanked together in a chatty way as I walked back to a small table in front of a window that seemed to peek up under the skirts of the hill that rose behind my father's house.

After arranging everything on the table I sat on a chair that looked into the heart of the kitchen and I watched Florence and my father prepare dinner. My father never used to cook in Iowa, but he was now in charge of all our salads. Right now he was mixing olive oil into lettuce leaves while searching the countertops for the bottle of vinegar he would use next.

Florence was bending over, reaching into the oven, pulling out the chicken. She was using the stained and frayed pot holders that I'd woven from many-colored loops of material when I was five or six years old. My father hadn't brought many things with him when he left Iowa, but he'd brought those.

"You don't seem too thrilled about going back," Florence said, standing and carrying the chicken to the table. "I've been wondering for days: How do you feel about it?"

I sat up straighter, tensing, not having expected her question. "I don't know," I said warily. Out of the corner of my eyes I saw my father stiffen too and look from Florence to me, his face troubled.

"Well," Florence continued, "I don't know about you, but we've had a wonderful summer. And it wouldn't have been nearly so wonderful if you hadn't been here." She glanced from me to my father. Their eyes connected and I saw the corners of my father's eyes pinch in warning. She leveled her eyes at me. "Have you considered staying here with us instead of going back?"

"Now, Florence," my father said in a tone of voice I hadn't heard him use all summer, but that he had often used with my mother. He was tossing the lettuce faster and faster. "I don't think we should be trying to influence Chester one way or the other. It's his decision and I don't think we should interfere."

40
▼

"Interfere?" Florence took a step back from the table so that she could easily see my father and me at the same time. Color was creeping up the sides of her neck.

"I'll admit that part of the reason I bring it up is selfish," Florence said, singing her words in monotone. "I would very much like Chester to remain a part of our lives."

"Florence . . ." My father's voice pleaded with her to stop.

"However, I think that there are other reasons to bring it up as well . . . less selfish reasons . . . reasons having to do with Chester and his happiness." She was addressing my father, but it was obvious that she was also talking to me. "You've been a gentleman all summer, Harvey. I know that this whole business of who Chester lives with is tearing you up inside."

My father opened his mouth to say something and Florence held up her hand and raised her eyebrows. "Let me finish. Please. You've been a *perfect* gentleman, not trying to influence your son one way or the other. But I think it's about time somebody asked Chester some questions that might help him make the right decision."

She faced me. I cringed, not wanting a lecture, not wanting her to make my leaving more difficult than it already was. "I'm not saying you should live here," she began. "But I think you need to answer some questions for yourself before you decide. Either way somebody's going to get hurt, and ever since I heard of this *silly* arrangement I thought it was a cruel and unfair thing to do to you."

She understood how I felt! I could hardly believe my ears!

"Now, wait just a minute." Florence and I looked at the hurt expression on my father's face.

"Don't get me wrong, honey," Florence said, her voice losing its edge. "You did what you thought was right at the time. But if you ask me, the whole thing sounds cooked up by some lawyer who thought it looked smart on paper. Well, it wasn't smart."

I almost clapped.

She turned back to me and I let my hands drop to my lap. "You don't need to answer out loud. But you sure better answer in here," she said, pointing at her chest. "Are you happy here in Santa Fe . . . with us?"

I swallowed, surprised by her bluntness, and nodded before I could stop myself. A smile flickered at the corners of her mouth.

"Are you happy back in Iowa?" She stared at me so hard, it almost hurt.

My face crumpled as the answer echoed in my head. The way I felt was so obvious that even José had asked that question—and knew the answer too.

She sat down in the chair next to mine. "Look, Chester. I know it's not easy, but you have to be honest with yourself, regardless of what you decide. I just have one more question and then I'll be quiet. Don't you think your mother would want you to be happy?"

I looked around the kitchen, trying to keep from looking into Florence's eyes. I don't know, I answered to myself. I—I don't know.

"Honestly!" my father exclaimed. "Look what I've

done!" He picked up a handful of bruised lettuce, dark and droopy as cooked spinach. It dripped a combination of oil and lettuce juice.

Florence laughed and her shoulders rocked as if she were dancing. "Enough. Nobody will ever call me Florence Nightingale!" She stood, pushing the chair away from her with the back of her calves and leaning over me. Kissing me on the forehead, she said, "Just so you know. We'll respect whatever you decide to do." And then she straightened, looking tall and strong and big as she stood in front of me. "Just remember, the choice is *yours*."

After dinner I climbed the hill behind my father's house to watch the sun set. I was confused, not sure if my thoughts and my emotions were in agreement. For the first time I was seriously doubting my decision to go back to Iowa. I felt a growing anger at my mother and father and at myself. Why should I have to decide where to live? I was the kid. They were the parents. It wasn't fair. Plus I couldn't find a thing wrong with what Florence had said before dinner. I wanted to be alone, to sort things out, to let my anger cool.

Sitting, I pulled my knees up to my chest, resting my chin on the groove between them. A band of clouds was blocking the sun, stretched across the western sky, hovering over the Jemez Mountains beyond the Rio Grande. As I watched, the sun's bottom appeared, igniting the belly of the clouds. Their towering heads darkened into smoke.

As the sun sank lower, I looked at the town of Santa

Fe. Windows were ablaze with the sunset's colors, making the houses on the hillsides look as if they were burning inside and were about to explode. Strings of streetlights came on, delicate as dew on a spiderweb.

The sun burned lower and the Jemez Mountains shimmered—a mound of coals that grew cool and dark at the base and still glowed on top.

It was an incredible show of light and space and distance—an amazing show of beauty—almost too beautiful, painfully beautiful, so beautiful that I discovered I'd been holding my breath. Gasping, trying not to make the sounds of crying, I turned my eyes away from the spectacle, unable to continue looking without shattering into a million pieces.

As I breathed deeply, slowly catching my breath, I looked down into the soothing, darkening shadows of the valley where my father lived. On the dirt road in front of my father's house sat a cat—black except for four white boots and a white triangle that spanned its chest and tapered downward, toward its belly. The Tuxedo Cat, I thought, dressed for a night on the town with his spats and a starched white shirt.

The cat sat perfectly still, except for the end of its tail flicking dirt. Its head was tipped up as it studied the wall separating the road from a neighbor's yard. And then suddenly, with no apparent effort, the cat sprang, barely clearing the wall.

As the cat's tail floated over the wall and disappeared, I clenched my fists and my eyes widened. How did the cat know that there wasn't a dog waiting on the other side of the wall? How did the cat know that there weren't rosebushes with thorns or broken glass from beer bottles thrown over the wall from passing cars and pedestrians?

My throat tightened as I thought of the hidden dangers on the other side of the wall. I hoped that the cat had known what was on the other side, that it wasn't hurt, that it hadn't jumped so beautifully into something dangerous—or deadly.

And then, beyond the wall, I saw a shape glide across the yard: four white dots moving, trading places in a line, disappearing into darkness.

▼▼▼▼▼▼▼▼▼▼▼

PART II

the streets laid
out in
neat blocks
the cars run on
the streets laid
out in
neat blocks
children sit
bored feet idle
lazy bored stiff
minds laid
out in
neat blocks

CHESTER HORNIG

FOUR

▼▼▼▼▼▼▼▼▼▼

From where I sat on the edge of my bed, I could look out my second-story window and onto the backyard. I didn't like what I saw. I'd rushed up to my room expecting to look out over the old familiar lawn, studded by spiky and rounded bushes and rimmed by flowers. I'd expected to look out at the familiar calloused trunks of oak trees whose crowns pushed away the sky and made a high-ceilinged, comfortable space below for moving around. Instead I found myself looking at a strange new swimming pool. Its water was the same blue as the sky back in Santa Fe. Trapped in a swimming pool the blue looked artificial and puny.

Why? I asked myself as I stared out the window. I don't even like to swim.

For some crazy reason my mother had torn up the

yard and built a swimming pool while I was gone. She hadn't told me about it, so I assumed that it was supposed to be a surprise. And around the swimming pool, where the bushes and trees had been, were brown scabs of dirt that looked as if they were prepared for grass seed. Under one of the missing bushes, a large forsythia, had been my metal box with notebooks of poetry and the magazines I didn't want anybody to know about. The magazines I could live without—I hadn't even thought about them during the summer . . . much. But the poetry was another matter. They were like a physical part of me, my brain's fingers and toes. And now they were gone.

I threw myself backward onto the bed. Looking at the shiny flecks in the white, textured ceiling, I found that I missed the honey-colored, rough-sawn beams and planks of my bedroom ceiling in Santa Fe. I took off my glasses, laid them on my chest, and rubbed my eyes. A warm, soothing feeling spread from my eyes down through the rest of my body. I breathed deeply. The air was still and cool—pasteurized, homogenized, smooth. Too smooth. After a Santa Fe summer of open windows and billowing curtains, it was strange to be sealed in a room, sitting in a square bubble of cooled air, separated from the outside by double layers of glass. I sat up and shivered—not entirely from the cold air that blew up from registers embedded along the walls in the pale green, sculpted carpeting.

I closed my eyes and thought back on my day. I pictured walking into the waiting area of the terminal and seeing my mother as if a spotlight was shining on her and the rest of the room was dark. I couldn't remember hearing any sounds, although the room must have been noisy with greetings and announcements coming over the public address system. My mother glowed with happiness when she spotted me—glowed in the same way my father had glowed the night before when I announced my decision. Her perfume triggered strong and dreamy childhood memories of smelling flowers to see which one was most like my mother. I'd never found a flower that smelled as good.

It was then, in the airport, that I realized how much I'd missed my mother over the summer. And now, remembering that, the sounds of the waiting room came back to me—a happy din, almost like cheering, that exploded in my head. I'd forgotten I was carrying a leather knapsack by its back straps and I reached out to hug her, almost banging her in the stomach as it swung beyond my hands.

She was surprised by this gesture, and her stiffness didn't entirely disappear as she hugged me back. "You!" she finally said, letting go and holding me at arm's length. She smiled and shook her head as if she were scolding me. "You grew up over the summer. *And* you need a haircut." She brushed the hair from my forehead and pushed my glasses up, all in one motion. She whispered in my ear, "I missed you, Chester. Terribly. Now"—she was suddenly all business, stepping away from me—"let's get your luggage."

I was instantly afraid. Hesitantly, I lifted the almost empty knapsack to my waist and quietly said, "This is all I brought."

My mother looked stunned, and I was certain that she now realized that I had come home to tell her I was going back to New Mexico. But then she smiled. It would have been so much easier if she'd just known.

"Clever boy," was all she said. As we walked toward the main lobby, she took my free hand and swung it back and forth in the embarrassing way of high-school sweethearts. "You wanted a new wardrobe for school, huh? Now we'll just have to shop. Shop till we drop!"

When we stepped outside, the hot and heavy air seemed as difficult to breathe as diesel exhaust. As always, my mother was driving a new car with dealer plates, and because she drove so many different cars, she didn't remember which one to look for or even where she'd parked it. While we paced up and down the parking lot, I felt as if I were being crushed between heat that radiated up from the asphalt and the heat that pressed down from the sky.

After a thorough tour of the upper lot, and noticing how many Chevrolets were sold by other dealers, we found the car—a bright red four-door. It was close to where we'd started looking. By then I felt as if I'd bathed that morning in curdled milk instead of soap and water.

I'd been dreading the drive from Des Moines to Clifton. It was during this ride that I'd planned to tell my mother I was going to stay a few days and then go back to Santa Fe in time to start school. But before I could say anything, my mother began filling me in on what had happened over the summer. I listened with a mixture of relief and irritation, alert for chinks or gaps in her conversation so that I could tell her my bit of news. But it had been an unusually interesting summer in Clifton and I didn't have a chance—especially not with the speed at which my mother talked.

Sissy Landry was pregnant but she wouldn't reveal the father and she wouldn't have an abortion. Even so, everybody suspected Horace Givens, the Methodist minister's youngest son, because he'd suddenly been sent off to live with an aunt and uncle in the Twin Cities. Just a couple of weeks ago somebody tried to rob the bank but the man was caught when he ran into the rope barriers that force people to form lines, got hopelessly tangled, and was pinned to the floor by Morris Foley, state AA bantamweight wrestling champion. Morris held him in a full nelson and gave an interview to a newspaper reporter until the police arrived.

As I listened, I looked back and forth between my mother and the gentle corn-covered hills outside. I couldn't help playing an old childhood game of mine: I looked over the tops of my glasses and imagined that the blur outside was a greenish, algae-filled lake and that the car was a boat and the hills were the waves that rolled off the wake of the parted water. The wind-tossed yellowish corn tassels were the spray coming off the bow of the boat.

I pushed my glasses up and was struck by how green and close everything was here—too green and too close. I found myself straining to look farther than the trees and corn would allow and thinking that the clouds I saw above them were distant mountains—shades of dark blue at the base and patches of dazzling white near their peaks. It was disappointing to remember that Iowa didn't have mountains.

My mother talked and talked, tidbits of news pouring out of her. She'd written me a couple of letters every week during the summer and she'd never mentioned anything as exciting as Wilmer Farmer having his appendix taken out or Jewel McCarthy, the girl next door, running away to find her biological mother. I hadn't even known Jewel was adopted.

While she chattered and drove, I took the opportunity to look at my mother's profile. The skin on her face was smooth and taut, seeming to make her jaw snap shut whenever she opened it. Her mouth was like a round rubber band stretching and releasing, words popping out fast and sharp. For some reason the skin on her face reminded me of too-tight jeans. As I watched her, I wondered why she hadn't told me any of this news in her letters. Had she been punishing me for being away? Was she now rewarding me for being back?

Clifton looked the same as always when we drove into town. An old tree by the bandstand in the park off Main Street had blown down in a thunderstorm. That was about all. Certainly the house looked the same as always as we went up the driveway. Its blank, closed windows gave me the same tight feeling inside as always.

And now I was inside that house, lying on my bed with my eyes closed, wondering if I'd ever have the guts to tell my mother what I'd come to say.

"Knock, knock."

I opened my eyes and propped myself up on my elbows. My mother stood in the doorway, blurry and faint. The pictures in my head are never out of focus, and it's always a disappointment to open my eyes and not see clearly. I felt around for my glasses, found them on my stomach, put them on, and blinked at the shock of everything coming into sharp focus. My mother's smile had a hint of mischief about it.

"I bet things look pretty different after being away for a whole summer." She was struggling to keep from looking out the window.

"Yeah." I played it cool, not wanting to acknowledge the swimming pool that shattered and scattered the sunlight in the same way that it shattered and scattered my feelings.

"It's still early in the afternoon. Maybe you should go out and mow the back lawn." She was struggling not to smile, and she held her arms around her chest as if she were trying to keep her excitement inside. "You've mown the lawn so often, I bet you could mow it with your eyes closed."

She was terribly pleased with herself and with her surprise, and she was dying to tell me. But I was feeling mean and looked at her with a frown, ready to prick her balloon, muddy her puddle, grease her mirror—whatever. "If I did that, I might fall into the swimming pool out there."

She stared at me for a moment, looking extremely disappointed, and I regretted spoiling her surprise. But she recovered almost instantly and began to laugh. "You little scamp! You knew and you didn't say anything!"

I grinned in spite of myself.

"What do you think of it?" She walked to the window and looked out. There was no question what she thought.

"It's"—I struggled to say what I knew I should say—"it's okay." I sounded flat and I tried to make up for it by snapping on an energetic smile as she turned to look at me, to test the honesty of my answer.

"Well, now." She walked over and sat next to me on the bed, craning her neck so that she could see the swimming pool from where she sat. "I had to practically use whips to get it finished on time, and I haven't let a soul use it since it was finished. I haven't even so much as stuck my own big toe into it. I was saving that for *you*."

My shoulders slumped before I could tell them not to. I knew what was coming next, and I didn't like it one bit.

"Why don't you put on your swimsuit and go on down there and try it out." My mother looked me up and down. "I declare! You've grown so *much* this summer." Leaning toward me, she whispered, "And if your suit's too small, don't worry. I made sure none of the neighbors could see the pool from their houses." She winked.

I'll bet Jewel McCarthy could find a way, I thought. I didn't want to go swimming at all, much less with nothing on. I was about to tell her that I'd swim in overalls first when, luckily, I remembered the present that I'd brought her. It, alongside a copy of *The Catcher in the Rye* and my toothbrush and toothpaste, was the only thing in my knapsack. I picked up the knapsack from where it sat at my feet and unzipped it.

"I brought something for you. From New Mexico." I drew a ball of paper from the bag and watched my mother unwrap it. At last she held in her hand a clay pot the size and shape of a tulip. It was reddish, with geometric designs in black around it that represented thunderclouds and lightning.

"It's darling," she said, slowly. "It's such a pretty thing. Now tell me: Where did you get this?" I could tell that she was being as careful as I'd been about the swimming pool.

"Under the portal at the Palace of the Governors," I told her, remembering the place and the time so well that for a moment I imagined myself kneeling in front of the colorful blankets spread out on the brick side-walk. I'd agonized between this pot and a pair of silver-and-turquoise earrings that sat so prettily on a square of black velvet. "You know, the one on the Plaza. I bought it from an Indian from the Santa Clara Pueblo."

She held it up level with her face and looked at it from all sides in a show of happiness. "It's just lovely. Thank you." Leaning over, she pecked me on the cheek. "I'll take it downstairs and put it on the mantel over the living-room fireplace. That way we can both enjoy it and it can remind you of your summer in Santa Fe."

My happiness instantly turned to disappointment. She was assuming that I was staying when, in fact, I was not. At least I hadn't been planning to stay. My whole body tensed as she stood and walked to the door. Turning around, she said, "Tell me if the water's too hot or too cold. That way we can have the pool man adjust it when he comes by tomorrow."

And then she disappeared from my room.

It was as if she'd taken the air with her. I began to shake with the anger that came every time I thought of my predicament, the decision I'd had to make. She was making it difficult to do what I had to do, to say what I had to say. She was boxing me in. She hadn't asked once about my summer or how I'd enjoyed Santa Fe. I hadn't expected her to ask me about Florence. But I had expected her to ask how my father was doing or if I had made any friends. Instead she'd kept the conversation focused on Clifton and on herself, making it impossible for me to tell her anything about my summer, about what I was thinking or feeling.

My father had been right. Last night he told me that I should tell her on the phone of my decision. He said that coming here to tell her was an admirable and grown-up thing to do, but that I didn't need to do it.

I hadn't listened. I'd said that I needed to come here— I had to tell her face to face, so that she could see how much I loved her even though I wanted to live with him. And with Florence. I told him I wanted to *show* her I wasn't rejecting her by choosing him.

I didn't lie to my father, but there was more to it than that. Just as important to me was retrieving my notebooks of poetry. They are part of me—my thoughts made visible. I had wanted to come back here to get them. But now there was a swimming pool where they used to be.

My father had been right—in more ways than one.

I stood by the side of the pool, my toes gripping the edge so tightly that each toe knuckle was white. Moments ago I'd touched my hands together over my head, getting ready to dive. But I'd let that moment pass and now I was hugging myself to keep from shaking apart, even though it was muggy and hot. I felt nervous and foolish standing by the pool in my suit that was so small, it hurt. And I felt vaguely dizzy without my glasses. Without them the cement I stood on looked soft and fuzzy enough to sink into.

I've never liked swimming. It isn't that I can't swim. Even though I don't swim as beautifully as my mother, I'm competent in the water. My problem is getting in the water, losing myself in something that swallows me whole. I don't like opening myself up to the cold. It would be different if I could be selective about what gets cold and what doesn't. I'd gladly get in the water if I could keep my face and feet and back dry and warm while everything else got wet. But I prefer being in control, being self-contained and drawn into myself. I don't like jumping into water any more than I like people yelling directly into my ear.

And another thing I don't like is not being able to see. I've tried several times to swim with glasses on. They won't stay on properly and they pull at my head in funny ways and the water sheeting off them makes everything blurry and squirmy anyway. Wearing them wasn't worth the bother. But without my glasses, everything in and around a pool looks as if it's underwater.

So there I stood, on the edge of the pool, in a growing puddle of sweat, knowing that my mother was watching from someplace, knowing that with every passing second her disappointment must be growing. I knew that I'd have to jump in sooner or later.

When I couldn't stand it any longer, I crouched and threw myself in, landing on a shoulder and yelling from the cold. I forced all the air out of my lungs and, kicking madly for the other side of the pool, pulled myself out with a grunt and threw myself onto the deck. I lay for a moment, my heart thumping hard and fast, breathing in gasps.

A blur approached the pool from the house. "How was it, Chester?" my mother called. And then the blur flung itself at the pool and disappeared in a tiny splash.

A head popped up next to me. "That felt wonderful! What do you think! Not bad for a late birthday present, huh?"

In my bedroom I stood by the window looking out at the backyard. It was growing dark and the swimming pool looked like a rectangular bruise in the lawn. I had a pad of paper in one hand and a pencil in the other. For the first time all summer I felt like writing some poetry. For the first time all summer I was retreating into myself, into that lonely place where my poetry comes from.

At dinner my mother had continued her one-sided

chatter. I was too tired and overwhelmed to take advantage of the pauses when she took bites of food or sips of wine. The more she talked, the less I wanted to say anything, the less I wanted even to look at her or nod and grunt at the appropriate times.

Finally my mother stopped her talking and stared at me. "Are you feeling all right?" she asked.

"I'm tired," I replied. And I was too.

"You've had a long day. Traveling is hard work. And we have a big day ahead of us tomorrow. You need clothes and supplies for school. And I think it's about time to look into getting a computer for you."

I didn't agree or disagree with her. I was tired and I felt defeated. I nodded and began to gather up my plate and silverware and glass to take into the kitchen.

"Don't worry, Chester. I'll take care of that."

Don't worry. What a thing for her to say, I thought bitterly, setting everything I held back on the table.

"Good night," she called as I made my way up the stairs. "Say your prayers." She hadn't said that to me in years. It sounded funny and out of place.

And now I stood in my bedroom, looking out the window. I was furious with my mother. She was doing all of this on purpose—avoiding the issue of where I was going to live—assuming that what *she* wanted was what *I* wanted. This way of pretending a problem didn't exist was dishonest. My father had played that game too. The only people who'd been honest with me about all of this had been José and Florence.

I pursed my lips in mockery. "Good night," I said, imitating her voice. "Say your prayers." I hadn't said my prayers in years. I had grown to feel that prayers were more for the person who was praying than for God—whoever He was. It was too much like having a conversation with a dial tone.

My fingers gripped the pencil as I lifted up the darkening white of the paper. "Say your prayers." I lowered my head, picturing my mother, bending closer to the dimming page. I could no longer see the ruled lines of the paper, so I wrote in large, loopy letters:

> *And when to yourself*
> *You pray each night,*
> *Beg forgiveness for the*
> *Words that make*
> *My eyes cry blood.*
> *My heart pumps tears.*

FIVE

▼▼▼▼▼▼▼▼▼▼▼

I woke up grumpy. Having had vague, horrible dreams and having slept badly, I kept my eyes closed for as long as I could and tried to clear my mind. When I finally opened them, I scowled at the room, my bad mood as blurry and unfocused as my sight.

I'd often felt like a guest in my own bedroom. My mother continually redecorated it—changing the wallpaper, buying new sheets to match, hanging various paintings on the walls that she thought would help me develop a fine taste in art. And it was always as tidy as a hotel room. Several years ago I went through a stage in which I tried to leave the biggest mess I could every morning before I went to school. I wanted to make my mark on the room, to make it mine. But every afternoon when I came home from school the room would be spotless and picked up, all traces of me gone along with the wadded tissue in the wastebasket.

I listened to the dead silence, thick as fog in my sealed bedroom, and wondered in a dull way if I could really tell my mother I'd decided to live in New Mexico. The longer I waited, the more difficult it was becoming.

The curtains were drawn but sunlight leaked in from around their edges, making pipe shapes down the wall from each rounded fold at the bottom. The light in my room was dead and flat, unlike the northern light that came through my bedroom window in Santa Fe. All the light in my father's house comes from the north, because the hill behind it blocks most southern light. It's a gentle light to wake up to, a light that is full of the fresh morning smells of dew evaporating from blades of grass and full of the sounds of birds. Florence says that the northern light is perfect for her work, because it brings out the colors in her oil paintings. She's right. Light from the north deepens colors, like splashes of water on cloth.

I wished more than anything that I were back in New Mexico, waking up to that light.

Without looking I groped around the nightstand for my glasses. I found them on top of the notebook that contained my poem from last night. I slipped on my glasses and felt more awake now that I could see clearly. My thoughts were sharper, and my feelings about being here and wishing to be back in New Mexico were sharper too. I reached for the notebook, flipped over onto my stomach, and stuffed it under my mattress as far as my arm would go.

Getting up, I walked to the window, fumbled with the draw cord, and yanked. The curtains snapped open and sunlight seemed to smack me in the face.

Outside, the pool's water lay perfectly still, its surface glassy and smooth. Held in its rectangular band of white cement decking, it was too flawless to be a stone of turquoise sitting in a silver setting. It looked like a chunk of transparent blue plastic sitting in putty.

I walked to the closet, thinking about what I should wear. I didn't know how hot it was outside—it always looks cool from inside an air-conditioned house. Opening the closet door, I was surprised and a bit angry to see that the clothes inside were arranged differently from when I had left earlier this summer. I slid hangers back and forth, looking for one of my favorite polo shirts. It was gone—of course. My mother often had our maid, Bertha, tidy up my closets. And each time, my mother allowed Bertha to take some clothes for her children, if my mother considered them worn out. In place of the polo shirt were several others I'd never seen before. I grabbed one, its price tag fluttering in the air. As always, I was furious that my mother would allow Bertha to take something of mine without first asking me and that she would buy me clothes without my approval. A pair of shorts I wanted to wear was also missing, along with my old lawn-mowing sneakers that were stained a mellow yellow-green. I'd always thought they were too ratty for Bertha's kids. Perhaps my mother had thrown those out herself.

I got dressed and walked down the stairs to the kitchen. The house was quiet and I wondered if my mother was up. Sometimes she spent much of the night drinking wine or Scotch, and reading or sitting in the back patio staring at the stars. After such a night she usually slept until noon or after.

"Good morning!" my mother announced, looking up from her newspaper and smiling at me, alert and perky. She was in the breakfast nook of the kitchen—a corner that was rounded like a tower and wrapped with plate glass windows. "What can I get you for breakfast?"

I shrugged.

"Would you like some toast? I have some wonderful raspberry jam to go with it. Or maybe I should skip the toast and just give you a spoon for the jam?"

I smiled in spite of myself. I love jam—especially raspberry. Toast is only an excuse to eat it, piled high on top of lumps of butter too big to melt before the toast cools. I forced the smile into a frown. "Toast would be fine. And a little jam."

"Good. Sit down. Here's the newspaper. I thought a few of the funnies were especially good this morning."

I sat down in the chair opposite the one my mother had been sitting in. Sunlight drifted in through the glass panes, having first been filtered through the leaves of a giant oak tree outside. The light bounced dreamily around the breakfast nook and kitchen but didn't seem to settle on anything long enough to warm it.

I ignored the newspaper and instead watched my mother walk around the kitchen. She occasionally turned to look at me, as if she couldn't quite believe I was there. She was wearing a trim dress that looked cool and comfortable, with a subtle pattern of greens and blues that went beautifully with the morning light. I'd always thought my mother was pretty. She was much prettier than Florence, and I felt guilty for even thinking such a thought.

What is pretty, anyway? I asked silently, scolding myself.

"There you go." My mother walked toward me with a plate of toast in one hand and the jam pot in the other. She set these things in front of me and sat in her chair. "Eat up. We have a big day ahead of us."

I piled jam onto the first piece of toast and sank my teeth into it. My mother grinned.

"I have an appointment for you at ten to get your hair cut," she said. "Or shall I say 'styled'?"

My enthusiasm for jam and toast instantly dimmed as she talked. I didn't want to get a haircut. With shorter, neater hair I might fit in better in Clifton, but I would look odd in Santa Fe. I didn't want to go back looking like a *turista* from Texas or the Midwest.

I swallowed. "I don't want a haircut."

My mother looked at me for a moment, her eyes narrowing, deciding whether or not to ignore that comment. "You must get it trimmed, at least."

"I don't want it trimmed." I knew I was beginning to sound belligerent, like a three-year-old, but I didn't care. For the first time in my life I felt like fighting her about how I looked—my hair and my clothes. I didn't want to give in one more time. Especially since I wouldn't be living with her.

This time she chose to ignore my comment. "And then after your haircut," she said, "I thought we should drive down to Des Moines for a little lunch at Bishop's and do some shopping for school. I heard from Larry's mother that Younkers has some wonderful prep clothes on sale."

I licked the jam off my lips and put down my piece of toast. My mother was stacking her hopes higher and higher, and in the process she was boxing me in. I was beginning to feel trapped, claustrophobic. I needed to punch out of this wall while I could still see over the top, and the only way I could do that would be to tell her of my decision to go back to New Mexico. It was now or never. I felt it, deep in my gut, and I swallowed hard.

But before I could say anything, my mother continued. "And I think we should go to the new computer store by Drake University and look at computer systems for you. Books are becoming obsolete, you know. At least that's what some people are saying. And besides, maybe you can teach me how to use a computer. They say children learn to use them more easily than adults. I believe it has something to do with old dogs learning new tricks."

I just stared at my mother as she strung her words tighter and tighter, leaving no gaps through which I could sneak through. It occurred to me that my mother must have known that I was going to say something she didn't want to hear. Her timing was too perfect.

"Mom, I—"

"Oh, I know," she interrupted, speaking more loudly than she needed to. "It'll be expensive." She held up a hand to keep me quiet and shook her head so that

▼

her curls bounced slightly, girlishly. "But I think any-body who doesn't have a computer in this day and age is handicapped. And if we're going to get one, we might as well get the best."

She'd stolen my moment. Her wall of hope towered over me. I felt trapped. I wanted desperately to get away from her.

I pushed my chair back from the table, angry and hurt. My mother looked up at me, startled.

"Did I . . ." Her voice trailed off, never becoming the question she intended.

I avoided looking at her.

"Chester, dear . . ." And for the first time since I'd been home, my mother sounded unsure of herself. But she recovered quickly. "You really should finish your breakfast. We have a big day ahead of us." She was beginning to repeat herself.

Without another word I turned and walked toward the patio door that led to the backyard. I didn't trust myself to say anything. What I had to say should be said well, should be said at the right time and in the right way. I didn't want to hurt my mother, but she was making hurt almost unavoidable. She wasn't giv-ing me a chance to tell her that I loved her even if I couldn't live in Clifton and be happy.

"Chester," she called, "be back by nine-thirty. It takes a little while to get downtown, and I don't want to be late for your hair appointment."

I opened the door and walked into a wall of hot air. It was thick and clammy, almost musty, as if I were breathing in air that had been breathed by somebody else. Walking by the pool, I swung around the house and cut across the yard toward the street.

I was hungry. I'd been walking for hours—tramping through the woods in the valley of the Skunk River, walking the streets laid out in neat blocks through Clifton, feeling as if I was walking on a grid: back and forth, zigging and zagging, left, right, left, right. I'd circled the elementary school I'd gone to—the one my mother and father had gone to—and walked past the junior high that was brand new last year. I'd walked up and down Lincoln Way and past my mother's car dealership with its little triangular flags of many colors flying and the front row of cars with their hoods open, showing off their clean engines. I thought about how much Arturo would have loved looking at them.

I was thirsty too. I'd hit every water fountain in town, but mine was the kind of thirst that no amount of liquids could satisfy. It was the thirst of an Iowa summer, a thirst one couldn't escape even by drowning in a cow pond.

I peered at my watch through streaks of sweat that had run from my eyebrows and down my glasses. Three oh seven, it said, but I wasn't sure if my watch was reporting Mountain time or Central time. I couldn't remember if I'd changed it since yesterday. I decided that I probably hadn't, which made it after four o'clock in the afternoon.

Oh well, I thought, shaking my head. I'd definitely missed my hair appointment. I'd missed lunch at Bishop's. I'd missed shopping for school clothes and buying a computer system.

I didn't regret those things. In fact, I was rather proud of myself. I'd never done this kind of thing to my mother before—stood up to her like this.

Right now I was only a couple of blocks from home. Within minutes I could be there, apologizing to her. I knew I'd have to apologize sooner or later, whether I wanted to or not. But the thought of facing her sent a chill up my spine, and spinning on my heel, I walked in the opposite direction with renewed energy.

Saying good-bye to Clifton hadn't been as difficult as I'd thought it would be. I figured that part of the reason was that I'd been saying good-bye so much lately that I was becoming almost professional at it. And I figured that the other part of the reason was that I wanted to say good-bye to Clifton. It felt like the right thing to do.

Several times during the day I'd wondered what José would think of my hometown. When I thought of José, I was surprised to feel almost homesick—homesick for Santa Fe. And thinking about what José would think made me see Clifton as if through his eyes.

He would have liked all the white clapboard houses, with their porches and all their bushes gathered around them in tight patches around front stoops—like fur collars. He would have enjoyed the lushness that didn't hide behind adobe walls, that spilled out everywhere, mixing one lawn with the next. He would have liked Boyd's Dairy, where Mr. Boyd made the best malts in the world—malts so thick, you'd suck your mouth inside out before you'd get anything up into the straw. Mr. Boyd also made his own ice cream and often came up with outrageous flavors. Dill pickle was one of the most memorable, even if it hadn't been among his best. Personally I thought his peanut-butter-and-grape-jelly ice cream was outstanding, and I suspected that José would have preferred Boyd's honeydew sherbet. I would have liked to go in and sample whatever new flavor Mr. Boyd had, but I'd left my money back in my bedroom and I didn't want to go back home and risk seeing my mother.

And I thought José would like Brookside Park, with its playground and its nature trails in the woods along the Skunk River. I'd outgrown the playground—today the elephant slide where I used to ride the rippling top of the trunk was too narrow for my rear end, and the whirling carousel made me so dizzy, I almost got sick.

As I walked through the park, I remembered the great flood that had happened when I was four or five. The Skunk River had swelled, angry-seeming and boiling with mud, until the water was so deep in the park that people canoed between the trees and the floating picnic tables, their corners partly submerged where they were held down by chain tethers. Now many of the large trees had died of Dutch elm disease and the ground was baked where shade had once protected thick patches of grass and violets and Solomon's seal.

I thought about such things as I walked along, my head bent forward and my hands jammed into the pockets of my shorts. I was so deep in thought that I almost ran into a little boy, maybe five or six, who was walking along the sidewalk ahead of me and going in the same direction. I pulled up and lagged behind before he knew that he was being followed. From the way he was walking, I suspected that he was angry or upset about something.

Sure enough, the boy began to take giant, exaggerated steps and to stomp his feet on the squares of cement that made up the sidewalk. He took two steps for each square, missing the cracks that divided them—but just barely. And then he began to mutter. I had to listen carefully from four squares back to understand what the boy was saying.

"Step on a crack. Break your mother's back. Step on a crack. Break your mother's back." The boy's voice got louder and louder with each step and his feet got dangerously close to the cracks but never stepped on them.

I hung behind, listening, an anger growing inside me as the boy's voice grew louder and angrier. "STEP on a crack. BREAK your mother's back. Step on a CRACK. Break your mother's BACK."

The boy came to a corner and continued across the street, going straight. Moments later, when I reached the corner, I stopped and stared after him. His voice grew fainter and fainter but didn't lose any of its anger. From where I stood, I couldn't tell if he was stepping on cracks or not. But the farther away he got, the more it looked as if that's what he was doing.

"Step on a crack," I said to myself, enjoying this old rhyme, watching the boy disappear around the next corner. "Break your mother's back."

I quivered inside with growing anger. I was angry with my mother. I was furious. I'd tried all day to avoid being angry with her and to avoid her anger by running away from her and from her trap. I knew that I couldn't keep running, that I'd have to face her sometime. Turning around and walking toward my house, I began saying those words out loud. They were powerful and terrible words and they felt wonderful to say.

"Step on a crack. Break your mother's back." I stomped each foot onto the sidewalk, getting closer and closer to the cracks that divided the squares. "STEP on a crack. Break your mother's BACK." With each step my blood ran hotter and my heart beat faster. "Step on a CRACK. BREAK your mother's back." It was exhilarating. The power I felt was almost unbearable.

Clenching my jaw and making a fist so tight that my fingernails dug into the palms of my hands, I stomped on a crack.

"STEP on a CRACK." My head felt giddy and my body felt light. "BREAK your mother's BACK." I stomped on another crack and the arch of my foot tingled.

The power! The hatred! The revenge! I stomped faster, working myself into a frenzy.

"Step on a crack! Break your mother's back!"

Over and over I stomped on the cracks. Harder and harder, until the jarring hurt my knees and made my thighs quivery and the soles of my feet ache.

Over and over I stomped on the cracks, fury in my eyes, angrily breaking, breaking, BREAKING . . . my mother's back!

Breathless now, I came to the corner of the street where I'd lived my entire life—until this summer. I stopped, my chest heaving, my forearms hurting from clenching my hands so tightly. Throwing back my head, I stared at the sky fragments that were scattered among the tree leaves. My anger began to leak out and was replaced with fear. I couldn't put it off any longer. Taking one last, limp breath, I turned to my left and walked toward my house.

I was hot and sticky. My shirt felt stiff and abrasive from layers of crusty dried sweat that were slowly softening with this latest wave of sweat. Telephone poles marched down the street toward my house, and I noticed that partway down the block the lines strung between them disappeared. And then I noticed that the trees three houses down wore clouds of fuzzy green and that flowers were just gaudy splashes of color.

I wondered for how long I'd needed new glasses. Now that I knew this, I longed to see individual leaves in the distance, to see the numbers on the mailboxes two houses down—to see all of these things as clearly as I could see the cracks in the sidewalk at my feet.

And then a thought sent my brain aquiver. Talking to my mother was like using a telephone with no lines strung between the poles. In a rush I craved being able to communicate feelings to my mother as much as I wanted to see those stupid telephone lines.

As I walked along, going slower and slower, I felt

sick to my stomach about stepping on cracks and saying such a hateful rhyme. I shuddered, torn between wanting to continue down the street and wanting to turn on my heels and run as far away as I could—to never, never, *never* come back.

I forced myself to break into a trot. Soon I was running toward my mother's house. It was one of the bravest things I've ever done.

SIX

▼▼▼▼▼▼▼▼▼▼▼

The house came into sight, and as I approached, it grew as large as my fear. It sat comfortable and smug among the trees of our front yard, looking cool and satisfied. To catch my breath I slowed to a walk at the driveway. I felt sticky and hot and tired and smelly.

The red car my mother had picked me up in was parked in front of the closed garage door. I didn't know what to make of that. My mother almost always drives her cars inside—she hates getting into a hot car and the garage is air conditioned, just like the rest of the house. I approached the front door reluctantly, walking as if the soles of my shoes were sticky with tar. I pushed my glasses to their proper place and then opened the door slowly.

The door's bottom edge swished over the carpeting,

seeming to shush me. The air I stepped into was cold enough to make me shiver.

I crept through the foyer and through the living room. I heard nothing and saw nobody. I was getting a little spooked as I entered the dimness of the formal dining room. Its crystal chandelier looked icier than usual as it hovered over the long dark table. Still I saw nobody. I stepped into the brightness of the kitchen. My mother wasn't there. I was beginning to relax, thinking that my mother was probably upstairs in her bedroom, perhaps in bed, perhaps at her desk. And then I looked out the French doors that led to the backyard and sucked in my breath.

My mother was slumped in a lawn chair, facing the pool. A bottle of Scotch sat next to her, its nose pointing off at a drunken angle. The bottle was almost empty, and one of her hands was raised to eye level and holding a half-filled tumbler. Her head was turned so that she seemed to be peering at the world through the bevels of the heavy glass. I grasped the door handle and cranked, pushing at the same time. As I stepped into the backyard, I saw my mother's back stiffen. The hand holding the Scotch began to tremble and she lowered it haltingly until it rested on the arm of her chair.

As I walked toward my mother, my legs felt as if they'd lost their bones. I made a wide circle and stood in front of her, a little off to the side. She didn't look at me. Instead, she stared at the pool. Her mouth disappeared as she pressed her lips together, and her chest rose and fell more quickly.

And then she closed her eyes, saying, "You plan to

go back to New Mexico." Her words were crisp and she spoke with authority.

I was stunned. How did she know?

As if she could read my thoughts, she continued. "Your father called to ask when he might expect to meet you at the airport." This time her words came out slightly blurred.

My mother opened her eyes, and I saw that they were red rimmed and that she'd worn all the lipstick off her mouth from grinding her lips together, which she did when she was upset. The skin on her face was looser and paler than this morning. She looked now as she often looked before she'd wakened up properly.

"Tell me." She glared in my direction, not quite connecting with my eyes. "Tell me to my face. I want to hear it from *you*, not—*not* from somebody else." Now she sounded drunk and I didn't know what to say. I felt miserable and I wished now that I'd told her—just interrupted her and told her—flat out—not waiting for the right time, for the right words. It would have been so much better than this. But all my life I'd waited until the right time, until she was in the right mood, to tell my mother important things. Otherwise she'd always ignored what I had to say.

"Coward." My mother forced the word out like a cough, looking down at the Scotch that now stormed in her glass, waves licking the rim and leaving sheets as it fell back onto itself.

"Mom . . ." The word came out of my mouth, popped like a soap bubble, and disappeared. My mother's eyes flashed toward me, and they were hot with anger.

"I don't mind that you missed your hair appointment or that we didn't go to Des Moines . . . on our little shopping trip." Her lips and mouth were moving more than usual, and her words were coming out shrill and sloppy. "I don't mind that you never called me or that I drove all over this stinking little town looking for you." She shook her head and slowly raised the glass to her lips. She sipped, swallowed, and shuddered, her neck tightening and showing ropes of muscle and wires of tendon under her skin.

"I was worried, Chester. You've never done this before and I was worried. Worried sick. I had all kinds of visions." She was drawing me in, closer and closer, and I found myself letting her. I felt like a hooked fish being played with, pulled in. "I looked for you . . . at the bus station and . . . by the road and—and everywhere. Everywhere." She was sliding the net under me and was about to jerk me out of the water. "I guess I care too much about you, Chester. Too much. It's so hard!" she moaned. "Hard, hard, hard, hard . . . hard! I should care less. I should worry less. Less. Less." This last word hissed at me.

I was out of the water and she was gutting me. It hurt. It hurt enough to make me cry out. "Don't!" I was quivering and the pain in my voice startled her. She looked at me warily.

Her hands still shaking, she took another slow sip of Scotch, never taking her eyes off me. "Don't *what?*" she asked sharply.

"Don't—don't *do* this!" I sobbed. Tears sprang to my eyes and I angrily tried to get rid of them, shaking my head so hard, my glasses flew off my head and landed in the grass at my mother's feet.

With effort she bent over and picked them up with her free hand. She inspected them for a moment, frowning, and then held them out to me.

Not trusting my feet to move, I leaned forward and grabbed for them. I put them on and, to my amazement, saw that tears were running down her cheeks also.

"Chester, I wish you had told me yourself," she said in a voice that was thick. "It was such a shock . . . hearing it from your father . . . like *that*. Such a shock!"

"But, Mom, you never gave me a chance!" I gulped air. "I wanted to tell you, but you never stopped talking. You knew all along! I bet you knew all along . . . that I wanted to go back."

She winced and I knew I was right.

"You can change your mind," she finally said, looking at the Scotch as if she were studying a problem. "I was hoping that you would change your mind. That you would realize how much more you have here than your father could provide for you . . . for you in New Mexico."

Maybe it was walking around all day without anything to eat and not enough to drink. Maybe it was my mother's drunken anger. Maybe it was *my* anger. Maybe it was the relief of finally getting everything out in the open. Whatever it was, I felt dizzy and I closed my eyes hoping that it would go away. Instead I began to tip more to the side. I opened my eyes and reached out my arms to steady myself . . . too late. I took several wobbly steps to regain my balance and stepped right into the swimming pool.

My glasses washed over my head and my shirt billowed up with trapped air. The water was cold and I gasped, forcing air out of my lungs, making me sink faster. I pushed off from the bottom and my shorts dragged down, almost past my hips. As my head punched up through the water, I sputtered and swam in the direction I was facing.

"Over here," my mother called from my back. There was grim laughter in her voice. My clothes fought my every movement and I turned around with effort. Water ran from my hair and into my eyes, stinging with the salty sweat it scoured from my face. Without my glasses everything looked like splotches of light and color—mostly green.

I swam until I touched the wall of the pool. My mother reached for me, but before I saw her hand, I'd pulled myself up onto the pool deck with a grunt. Water sheeted from me.

I looked up at my mother as she leaned over me, unsteady on her legs, weaving back and forth like a boxer. She was smiling and still held the glass in her hand. It was empty now—she'd either spilled the rest or gulped it down.

"Here," she said, handing me the tumbler. And then, to my amazement, she did a perfect dive into the pool, barely disturbing the water. Her dress flowed back, almost like a cape, and the heels of her white pumps pointed upward like the rudders of two airplanes—only, they were flying backward. Totally amazed, I watched her wavery outline as it skulked across the pool bottom. At last she surfaced and swam the breaststroke toward me, my glasses held in her teeth. Her hair was slicked back, making a tight cap on her head, and her face wore a smile that reminded me of a dog's, swimming to shore with a stick in its mouth.

She pulled herself out of the pool so gracefully that she looked almost as if she had bounded off the top step of an underwater staircase. I stood and traded her my glasses for the tumbler.

"Nice move, Chester," she said, dripping water on the deck. "Nice move." She looked awake now, and her words were no longer as slurred. Water ran down from her hair and off her face like tears. It was an illusion—her face wasn't sad, just grim, and her eyes were hard. Her dress clung to her like tattooed skin, the cloth pulled into the lace of her bra.

"Bring that chair over here," she said, nodding to a second pool chair near the one she'd been sitting in. I saw goose bumps on her arms. "And then I want you to hear me out. Don't make up your mind until you hear what I have to say."

I did as she directed, and when I sat down she was still collecting her thoughts. Finally she looked up. "Maybe I am a little late but I was hoping to celebrate your birthday with you this evening . . . here . . . by this pool . . . just the two of us. You're a teenager! And I wanted to surprise you with a trip I've been planning in my head all summer."

Already my wet clothes were losing their coolness and growing warm and uncomfortable.

"I think it's about time you traveled, saw that the world is round and that there are other ways of living besides the way we live here in this little burg." She reached down and grabbed the Scotch bottle by its neck, throttling it, and tipped the last of the liquid into her tumbler. She looked back up at me.

"I was thinking of taking you out of school for a month or so and traveling through England and France." She studied me for a reaction, knowing that I had wanted to visit England and France for as long as I could remember. I pinched my face together to hide my surprise. It was a bribe, and I was tempted and revolted at the same time.

"I was also thinking of spending several days in New York City on our way back, seeing the sights, taking in some plays and a concert or two."

My mother knew how much I'd dreamed of going to New York, where I imagined the streets are filled with millionaires and writers and actors and musicians and poets and artists. She was hitting below the belt.

She waited for me to say something. I just looked at her and she looked at me. Our gazes didn't waver. I felt that we were playing a game of "chicken," our thoughts driving right at each other, fast and deliberate, and that neither one of us was going to swerve to avoid a collision.

She blinked first and cleared her throat. "As I said before, I don't think your father can afford to give you the things you need. He can't afford to give you a computer system, for example. He's poor, Chester, very poor, and he lacks any kind of ambition to better himself. He's poor and I'm rich. Rich, Chester. Think about it."

I thought it stunk. She'd never apologized about being rich, which was right. How can you apologize about being rich any more than you can apologize for being smart or good looking? Even so, she'd never stated it so baldly before. It was an ugly way of describing something beautiful.

"Someday all the farms and the car dealership and my place on the board of directors at the bank will be yours. Whether you want them or not, they'll be yours. And, believe me, those things will *not* move to Santa Fe to be near you. You will have to be here . . . here in Clifton . . . to make the most of them. You can't run away from them, Chester. You can't get away from them by moving down to Santa Fe . . . to live with your father."

I couldn't believe what I was hearing. But before I could argue, she continued.

"And another thing. I don't think it's fair for you to make a decision about this . . . about where to live . . . after spending the whole summer down there with— with *them*. I'm sure they showed you a good time and doted on you and made you feel that Santa Fe is the most exciting place in the world. And it *is* pretty special. But vacationing there for a summer is *not* the same as living there. I'm sure they made you feel that they would be miserable without you. I'm sure that—that woman . . . *Florence?* . . . that she has your father wrapped around her little finger. And"—my mother's voice was rising, a bitterness creeping into these words that made my ears cringe—"she probably *poisoned* you with evil thoughts about me. I don't deny that I have my faults. Nobody's perfect and I'm not even close. But I'm your *mother*, the one who *bore* you, the one who would give her *life* for you. And for some *Bohemian* . . . some gypsy *artist* . . . to badmouth me, telling you things that aren't *true* . . ."

I grabbed the arms of the chair and leaned forward. "That's a lie!" I shouted. "You don't know what you're talking about!" My mouth was a weapon, and I was shaking with anger. "How can you say that about Florence!" My voice was beyond shouting. It was that strained sound that animals make when they are startled, insulted, scared, and angry at the same time. "She *never* says bad things about you. She *never* tells my father what to do. My father *never* tried to get me to stay. He was a *perfect* gentleman." Florence's words packed a lot of satisfaction.

My mother sat straight up in her chair. "You can't tell me they didn't try to convince you to stay. I'm not *stupid*." Her voice was an echo of mine, fainter and lower, but just as angry.

"I didn't say you were stupid." I could feel my anger slipping away, and as if it had been propping me up, I slumped back into the chair. "I don't think you know how hard Florence tried to make me think about *me* . . . not you . . . not Dad . . . not her. But *me*. You're nothing but a . . . a *selfish* old . . . old woman!"

My hands trembled the way I've seen old people's hands tremble, and my head wobbled back and forth. My mother was shocked. I'd never spoken to her like that before. Never. Her eyes were wide and staring and her mouth was slightly open. When she finally spoke, she reminded me of the way I sound after I'm scolded.

"Chester, I . . ." She swallowed and began again, more loudly. "Chester, I just want what's best for you."

I knew she believed that. But there was more to it than that. She also wanted what was best for her. She was used to getting what she wanted.

"Then let me go back to New Mexico," I said quietly. And suddenly I wanted to share with her all of those things I loved about New Mexico that she hadn't given me a chance to tell her about. Words poured out of my mouth. "I have a friend there, named José, and we're going to go to the same school. And he has an older brother, Arturo, who's fixing up a car and making it into a low-rider. And there is a hill that's like a bald head in the back of Dad's house that looks over the whole city and you can see mountains everywhere and clouds being born and *everything*. And I can help Dad in the bookstore and read in my spare time and learn how to use his computer. And the Fiesta is going to happen in a couple of weeks and they burn a giant papier-mâché puppet called Zozobra and there are parades and everybody sings songs in Spanish and Don Diego de Vargas comes riding through on a horse."

I stopped. My mother looked as if she was going to get sick. Instead, she dropped the tumbler to the ground and held her arms out to me. Her face began to break up and her mouth gaped.

"Come here!" she cried.

It was as if my body moved of its own accord, but

I'm glad that it did. I got up and I went to her. She pulled me down on my knees and cradled my head in her arms. Her chair creaked and groaned and I was certain that it would collapse. My mother's arms held me tightly—too tightly—and she stroked the back of my head, bumping into the collar of my shirt with each stroke. Her chin knocked against the top of my head in a steady beat. Either she had the hiccups or she was crying. I was pretty sure I knew which, because I was doing the same thing.

▼

SEVEN

▼▼▼▼▼▼▼▼▼▼▼

We huddled for a long time, my mother's chin finally resting on top of my head. My mother's hold grew more relaxed as our crying ground to a halt. When I'd calmed down I got up, my legs unsteady, and stepped backward until I felt my lawn chair on the back of my legs. I sat down and looked at my mother, her head bowed and her shoulders hunched.

The light grew longer and dusk came, settling over everything like black Iowa dirt, muffling colors and sounds. Even the smell of dusk was that of damp Iowa soil. I looked from my mother and saw that a darkness was growing in the pool, as if ink had been released at the bottom and was slowly spreading upward and out.

Looking up at the tops of the trees marking the back of the yard, I saw that there were no trumpeting colors or bloodied clouds at sunset. The sun sank slowly, grand and proud, but also subdued and quiet and gentle, colors fading to gray almost as soon as they appeared. The sunset's lack of splendor and drama seemed appropriate—I felt that it was a near-perfect expression of the way I felt.

Mosquitoes broke the spell cast by the last light of the day.

"Ouch!" My mother jumped and kicked out a leg. The chair groaned as metal tubes strained. "I'm being eaten alive!" She spoke in her early morning, hungover voice.

I heard a persistent buzzing around my head. I hadn't heard that sound since the beginning of summer, since before I went to Santa Fe.

My mother reached down to swat at the mosquito on her leg. I heard the whap of skin on skin and another that sounded like skin on cloth. "Oh, dear," my mother said, lurching to her feet. "I'll be right back." And then she disappeared.

I swatted a mosquito that was drilling into my forearm, and a penny of blood appeared on my arm. I looked at the matching penny in the palm of my hand and then smeared both patches into my skin until they disappeared. Sitting in the lawn chair next to hers, I looked over the treetops. Stars were popping out of the night sky one by one and then began popping out in clusters. As I watched, I swatted and waved at mosquitoes. I'd grown up with this night sky, with these stars. They were familiar and comfortable and right, framed by the familiar shadows of the trees.

Stars in New Mexico are spectacular. They are clear and intense and there are more of them than in Iowa. But atop the hill behind my father's house I found it difficult to pick out the constellations—there were too many stars twinkling through the thin mountain air, which was confusing.

Here, in my mother's backyard, the Milky Way looked the way it should: It was a thin smudge that stretched across the sky, unraveling into nothingness along its edges. In New Mexico the Milky Way was a garish band of diamonds, glittery and seeming almost fake, like a dog collar covered with rhinestones.

I looked down and saw stars reflected on the swimming pool. The pool's water was glassy smooth and darker than the night sky, which made the stars shine more brightly at my feet than above my head. It was beautiful, and for a moment I forgot how much I disliked this pool.

I heard the clinking of glass on glass and looked up to see my mother half walking, half stumbling toward me through the shadows. The dark seemed as thick as a hedge, and she worked her elbows as if she were forcing back branches. When she got closer, I saw that one hand held a yellow-capped can of insect repellent and the other held a bottle of wine. Bouncing against the wine bottle were two upside-down goblets that sounded like glass bells every time they struck. She sat and placed the glasses and bottle carefully at her feet.

"Hold your breath and close your eyes," she said, leaning over and holding the can out to me. She pressed down and I heard the sound of spray, but I felt and smelled nothing. "Mercy," she sighed. I opened my eyes a crack and saw her take the can out of her right hand and rub her palm onto her leg. "It shot backward." I closed my eyes and she tried again. This time I took a deep breath and sat until I could barely hold it any longer. The mist was cool and prickly on my skin, and I opened my eyes to see if the cloud had gone away. I saw nothing but gray darkness. Before I breathed in, I quickly jumped up from my chair and took several steps toward the pool to get out of the cloud of spray. To my surprise I was still in a fog. And then I realized that my mother had sprayed my glasses along with the rest of me. I took a shallow breath, testing the air before I breathed deeply, took off my glasses, and rubbed the lenses on my shirt. The fog was gone when I slipped them back into place.

"Don't go falling into the pool again," she said, squinting through her own chemical cloud. "I don't want to go swimming right now."

I went back to my chair and sat. "Shouldn't we have dinner?" I asked, tipping my head toward the wine. I was hungry.

"Yes," she said, waving the mist away from her face. "In just a bit. But first I wanted to toast your birthday . . . and this new pool of yours—ours. I planned a celebration tonight and, by God, we're going to celebrate!" She sounded almost grim.

Expertly she opened the wine bottle, the cork making a wonderful cheek-stretching pop. The wine she poured into the glasses was as dark as the nighttime sky with occasional sparkles that could have been the fragments of stars.

We clinked glasses and she began to say something, but her voice was untrustworthy so she closed her mouth and flashed her teeth at me instead, watching as I took the first sip. The wine warmed my mouth, and a cloud of vapors rose from the back of my tongue and into my nose. I swallowed quickly and then sneezed, trying to be careful not to slosh wine from the glass.

When my parents were still married, they often allowed me to have a little wine with dinner. Unlike my parents I was a happy drunk, and they thought it was funny when I got giggly. This was the first wine I'd had for a long time, and it tasted good.

"Bring your chair closer, Chester." My mother beckoned with her hand as she spoke.

The chair's legs had sunk into the lawn, and it was somewhat like pulling dandelion roots to get them out so that I could move the chair next to hers.

When I was settled, she put her hand on my forearm and for a moment stroked the fuzz that passes as hair. I hadn't eaten anything all day, and after another sip of wine my head felt funny. I let my wineglass rest on the arm of the lawn chair, afraid to drink any more.

She turned to look at me. Her face was soft in the night light. The shadows on her face were black, giving her raccoon eyes. Her hair was still slicked down from when she'd jumped into the pool after my glasses. "Did I ever tell you that when I was about your age I'd sneak out of my house and into the night and talk to the stars?"

I raised my eyebrows in genuine surprise. "No," I said, leaning forward, eager to hear more. She hardly ever talked about her childhood, except the bad stuff.

"My parents . . . your grandparents . . . would have been shocked to know that their daughter was wandering around in the backyard in her nightie, letting fingers of the night breeze touch her the way she dreamed a man might touch her someday."

I know that when you become a teenager people start to treat you differently. But I wasn't ready for this kind of confession coming from my mother. She didn't sound drunk, but I looked at the wineglass in her hand and wondered how much Scotch she'd drunk before I got home—and how much wine before that. She didn't sound especially drunk, but these were unguarded words, drunk words.

"Yes," she continued dreamily, rocking the wineglass back and forth, making the wine swirl. "I would wander around our backyard and talk to the stars . . . and let them talk to me. Did you ever do anything—anything wonderful and crazy like that, Chester?"

I thought for a moment. "No," I lied, not wanting to share something like that with her. I hadn't exactly talked to the stars, but when I was younger I had imagined myself as a constellation, my stars strung together and moving like a marionette, trailing after Orion and drinking from the Little Dipper and riding the back of Taurus with the Pleiades, those seven sisters with their high, shimmering, starlike voices.

"That's too bad." She sounded genuinely sad, and

took another sip of wine. "In some ways you're just like your father." There was bitterness in her voice.

I was about to argue with her but decided against it. After all, she was right. In some ways I am just like my father. We keep our thoughts, our dreams, our poetry to ourselves. It's safer that way. My mother never understood that we needed to protect those tender and fragile parts of ourselves from her, that she would have handled them more roughly than they could stand.

"Oh, well," she continued, her voice once more dreamy and distant. "Then I would go back to my bed and be so wound up, I couldn't sleep. To help me fall asleep I'd lie in bed and close my eyes and pretend I was lying on clouds, towering clouds, piled high. And even though it was night down below, the clouds I was lying on were so high and so tall that the sun still shone on their tippy tops. And I would lie there and listen to the stars as they sang, singing me to sleep."

She sighed. I pictured what she described and a phrase came back to me, a phrase that had been born on top of the hill behind my father's house. *Pillow of clouds*. I stared at her in the dark, unable to see her mouth or the expression in her eyes. I knew she was watching me. I looked down from her face and saw her hand reaching toward me. I reached out and almost jumped as our fingers touched. Her hand took mine and it trembled faintly, like the light of a star.

She looked from me to the sky, her head moving back and forth as she scanned the heavens. "If you were going to pick out a star of your own . . . out of

all the stars in the sky . . . which star would it be?"
she asked.

I looked out over the trees. Orion is my favorite constellation. Even without my glasses I can usually pick it out by the linear smudge made by the three stars of Orion's belt. But tonight he wasn't yet visible. I looked over my right shoulder. "The star at the tail of the Big Dipper," I said. My mother squeezed my hand and the trembling stopped.

"That is a lovely star," she said, hushed. "*That* will be *our* star . . . the star that will talk to both of us . . . the star that will relay my thoughts to you and your thoughts to me"—her grip on my hand tightened— "while you're in New Mexico."

I had a hard time falling asleep that night. My mother and I had gone inside shortly after choosing our star. I showed her how I had learned to make a spaghetti sauce over the summer. I didn't tell her it was Florence's recipe, but I'm sure she knew—I certainly hadn't learned it from my noncooking father. We ate and she finally, dutifully, asked about my summer, wanting to know about José and what we did for fun.

I made her promise to come out to visit. She made me promise to write every week. We promised each other that we would communicate each Sunday night at ten o'clock through our star, letting the star at the tail end of the Big Dipper sing back and forth from New Mexico to Iowa so we would both know how the other was doing.

The night was surprisingly cool. A cool front must have pushed in from Minnesota or the Dakotas, which explained the crystal-clear sky—clear at least for Iowa. I forced open my bedroom window—it hadn't been opened for a long time—and enjoyed the feel of air slowly moving, seeming as restless as I was. The air wasn't as cool as in New Mexico, but at least it felt real. I closed my eyes and listened to the crickets and the faraway sound of a frog. An airplane cruised overhead, in the distance, its sound dragging on the earth's surface like an old rusty anchor. I was just about to fall asleep to these sounds when I heard the slap of footsteps on cement. I sat up and listened. The sound stopped, but not before I knew it came from the swimming pool.

Quietly I got up from bed and crept to the window and looked over the yard to the pool.

Standing by the pool was my mother, a pile of clothes off to the side. She stood by the pool, her back to me, her head bowed as she looked at the water. She was naked.

The pool was a mirror of the sky, so perfect that it looked like the sky itself. The stars were brilliant, some floating on the water, some seeming to shine from various depths within the water itself, winking and moving and winking again in slightly different places.

And then, as if in slow motion, my mother raised her arms above her head, and with incredible grace she dove into the sky, scattering the stars outward from an ever-widening circle of darkness. I turned from the window and walked back to bed. I wanted to watch my mother swim in the lovely pool of stars. I ached inside with the loveliness of what I'd seen.

But what my mother was doing was not done for my eyes or for any other eyes. She was celebrating life— her happiness, her sorrow—in her own way. I would have been ashamed of myself if I had not allowed my mother this pleasure—this very private pleasure.

I fell asleep to the sound of stars singing to me, feeling as if my head was floating on a pillow of clouds.

I left Iowa two days later. Looking back on it, I wish I'd left sooner.

As I was packing, my mother came into my bedroom so quietly that she startled me when I turned around and saw her standing in the doorway. I noticed her wry smile and saw in her hands the notebooks of poetry that I'd hidden under the bush in the backyard where the pool was now. I reached for them greedily. I'd never expected to see them again. Why had she waited until now to give them to me? I searched her face for the answer. And then she told me.

"I know it wasn't right, but I couldn't help reading them."

With my fingertips I explored the scuffed notebook covers that felt more like suede than cardboard, too shocked to be angry. In these notebooks were my most private thoughts and feelings, thoughts and feelings that made me embarrassed when *I* read them. In these notebooks were things too sensitive for anyone to know or touch.

"That's okay," I forced myself to say, a deep anger replacing my shock. I refused to look at her. I felt more exposed than if I'd been caught fiddling with myself. My worst fear, always, had been of people hearing my unguarded thoughts. And now she had read some of them in my notebooks.

"Those magazines are thrown away," she said, her voice taking on a scolding edge. To my anger was added shame—those magazines had been pretty raunchy. "Where did you get them?"

"The men's room at the showroom," I said quietly.

She raised her eyebrows as she thought of this. I knew she'd be visiting the men's room tomorrow. Then she looked at the notebooks in my hand. "You write well, Chester," she continued. "Your poems, especially, are beautiful. But they're so melancholy!"

I swallowed. And then I nodded. When I finally gathered enough courage to look up at her, she was gone.

Someday I'd like to write happy poems, I thought, to myself and to my mother. Someday I'd like to feel happiness as strongly as I feel sadness—and anger.

I was becoming an expert on the feelings of anger.

▼▼▼▼▼▼▼▼▼▼▼

PART III

Paint a picture of blue.
Blue sky blue
Hills blue sea
A wind blue
From the mountains.

And paint me in
The right hand upper
Corner a bird
Scanning the blue horizon.

CHESTER HORNIG

EIGHT

▼▼▼▼▼▼▼▼▼▼

I hadn't been gone a week, so I thought I'd be coming back to a familiar place. But in five days I'd forgotten almost everything. Santa Fe was brighter and louder and more beautiful than I remembered it. The sunshine seemed to shout with pleasure. The sky was an unbelievable blue. The clouds were fresh and new, not stale and mildewy like most clouds back in Iowa.

Even though I returned to New Mexico on a Friday, both my father and Florence met me at the Albuquerque airport—a friend of my father's sometimes babysat the store. I was so happy to see them that I whooped like a three-year-old and tried to hug both of them at the same time. Florence wept happy tears and my father cleared his throat continually as we waited for my luggage (mostly new school clothes from Younkers Department Store), watching the carousel go round and round in its hypnotic way, folding in on itself at the corners, fanning out on the straightaways.

The front wheels of Florence's car needed balancing, and they chattered along the highway as we left Albuquerque. It felt as if we were driving down a corrugated dirt road instead of an interstate. My father was hunched over the steering wheel, almost resting his chin on its top. Florence was turned in the front passenger seat so that she faced my father and the road at the same time, looking very proper, as if she were riding a horse sidesaddle. Her cheeks and smile bounced when we hit large bumps. Our conversation was simple, almost shy.

I sat in the back, like a paying customer, looking out the window, enjoying the bumpy ride, overwhelmed by the fact that I was actually in New Mexico—that this was where I now lived.

I felt as if we were flying rather than driving as we crested the final hill and descended into Santa Fe. The thick greenery of the city spread out in a fan shape, contrasting with the barren land around it, looking as if it had been washed down off the heavily forested Sangre de Cristo Mountains that towered above the city.

Florence turned to me and smiled. "Welcome home, Chester."

I looked from Florence to the rearview mirror and saw my father's eyes smiling at me. He winked and I winked back.

They'd fixed up the spare bedroom—cleaned out most

of the books and replaced the pull-out couch with a real bed. Other than that, my father and Florence expected me to decorate my own room and gave me fifty dollars with which to do it.

"Florence can take you to the flea market tomorrow morning," my father told me. "You can pick out some things to furnish your room with." I remembered my mother's words about my father being poor as I nodded and decided right then not to spend that money on myself. Besides, I liked the bedroom just the way it was—even the spiderweb (with its spider) in one corner where the walls and ceiling met.

I was unpacking a suitcase when José burst into my room.

"E-e-e-e!" he cried, jumping onto my back and throwing me face first into the pile of new Jockey shorts. José rolled off to the side and sat looking down at me, his face split with a smile.

I waited for him to tell me "I told you so," but he just burst out laughing instead. "Hey," he said, scrambling off my back. "Let's get out of here."

I felt guilty about leaving the house right away, especially after my father and Florence had made a special effort to pick me up. But as José and I walked into the living room, we caught Florence and my father kissing. They looked up, startled.

"Just practicing," Florence finally said, "for—"

"Let's wait," my father said gently, touching her mouth with his fingertips.

Florence nodded and quickly kissed my father's fingertips before she stepped away from him.

"Going off to see if Santa Fe looks different . . . now that it's your home?" she asked.

"If you don't mind. . . ."

"Of course we don't mind." My father's eyes twinkled and I wondered if they wanted to get rid of me so that they could continue "practicing." And then, as if he read my thoughts, he added, "Florence has to do some painting today for her gallery opening, and I should go off to the store. Come visit when you're finished exploring. I want your opinions on some children's books I've ordered."

"Off with you," Florence said, shooing us with her hands. "I *am* getting nervous about my opening." It was hard for me to imagine Florence nervous about anything. But it was her first opening and it was a big deal. "Oh. José? Would you ask your mother if you could join us for dinner tonight? But only if you'd like to."

"All right!" José almost jumped for joy. "Let's go, Chester." He pulled on my elbow impatiently.

I smiled my thanks to Florence. With a quick motion that made me think of her as a schoolgirl, she pulled her hair up into a ponytail and then let it fall, fanning against her back. She returned my smile.

We raced to José's house. Bracing myself for the shadow of the arch that guarded their driveway, I didn't flinch or stoop as we ran through it.

"I'll be right back," José called as he rushed into the back door, leaving me standing in front of the carport. Arturo's car was in the same spot as before, except now it was facing the other way. Had he gotten it running while I was gone? Arturo's head appeared from the side of the lifted hood, and he looked me over with a cool expression on his face.

"Hi," I said, feeling awkward as he stared at me.

"¡Hola!" he said, without enthusiasm. "So they kicked you out of Iowa and you landed here." One side of his mouth twitched with a sly smile.

"So your car isn't running." I surprised myself with this brave statement slipping out before I even knew I'd thought it.

Arturo grunted, and I was afraid I'd made him angry. Instead he smiled. "I thought I'd have it running by now. I almost got it a couple of times . . . once long enough to get it onto the street. We had to push it back." He shrugged. "Maybe I'll get it going before school starts. Maybe I won't. I've got to get the engine going good before I paint the body, anyway." He pulled a pack of cigarettes from a back pocket of his jeans. Taking a flattened, bent cigarette from the pack, he molded it into its proper shape and stuck it between his lips. "Got a light?" he asked, checking the pockets of his jeans.

Just then the door slammed open and José ran out to us, his arm still straight out from pushing the door. He stopped beside me, let his arm flop to his side, and stared at his brother. "Go ahead," he said. "Go ahead and smoke it. Just leave me your car when you die of lung cancer."

Arturo snorted. "I'll leave you the broken parts," he said. "What keeps happening to my matches?" Glaring at José, he stalked toward the house.

"I can eat with you," José announced. "Hey! It rained while you were gone. Want to see what's in the arroyo? I know where we can find a better car than that piece of junk."

Before Arturo could say anything, we scooted around the corner of the house. José jumped up, as if he were dunking a basketball, and whooped. "E-e-e-e, I got him!" he shouted.

I was tempted to imitate José's accent, to put words together the way he did. But I decided against it. It would have all sounded too weird. "Yes," I agreed. "You got him good, all right." I was bursting with joy, something that didn't often happen. "Race you!" I shouted, sprinting past José. I raced down the street, hearing him right behind me, but I cut the corner into our driveway so close that he couldn't pass me unless he went a longer way around. I reached the trail behind the carport just in time, just before I was about to collapse from this unusual effort.

I could barely make it up the hill. I stumbled several times and José skipped around me and beat me to the top. He stood waiting, his feet apart and his hands on his hips, looking down at me as if he were king-of-the-mountain. When I reached the top he turned and, without giving me a chance to catch my breath, started down the other side of the hill, into the arroyo.

This particular arroyo was deep and steep and narrow. When José first showed me the arroyo, I'd asked him how it was made. With a straight face he told me that this arroyo, like all arroyos, was an ancient path made over thousands of years by packs of coyotes running through the hills, hunting things to kill and eat. He pointed out the opening of a den that was dug into the side of the arroyo and showed me doglike tracks on the arroyo's floor as proof of what he was saying. He said that mothers warned their kids not to play in the arroyos because sometimes coyotes caught them and ate them. I half believed him—until the first heavy rain of the summer showed me how walls of raging, mud-thickened water carved these gashes in the earth. Sometimes the water runs fast enough to carry old refrigerators and tires and anything else people push over the edge to get out of sight. Other times it carries only mud and rocks and buries or unburies what is already there.

The high, sheer walls of this arroyo block out everything around it, including sounds, so that when I'm in it I feel as if I'm in the middle of a wasteland instead of in the middle of Santa Fe. This arroyo kinks every hundred yards or so, zigzagging its way through the old part of town, finally joining the Santa Fe River. After a rain the arroyo floor is clean and smooth and firm. It's a perfect place for kids to practice driving motorcycles and three-wheelers. We threaded our way between several braided tire-tracks.

My favorite place in the arroyo is a stretch that has a long, tear-shaped island off to one side, made by an old Model A Ford that was dumped there many years ago. The rusted, flaking carcass of the Ford is pocked with bullet holes, and everything that could be eaten by rodents or insects is gone. The car has been there long enough so that chamiso bushes and a couple of young elm trees grow out of its vacant windows from the inside.

As we walked to the car, we didn't see anything especially exciting or new. The rain had swept away much of the debris without bringing down anything to replace it with.

"Bummer," I said, kicking at a rock that sat in its own crater, hollowed out by the water piling up against it and then rushing around.

"Yeah." José picked up a pebble and threw it against the car. "Maybe next time."

We walked up to the car and peeked inside. I didn't expect to see anything in particular and was about to turn away when something caught my eye, back where the trunk used to be. There I saw a pile of magazines, and the cover of the top one gave its contents away. The woman had cleavage like the Grand Canyon.

"Hey, José. Look what's in there." I started to crawl through the car's open front window. I handed a glossy magazine to José, being careful not to touch the woman and man on the cover in their private places. I watched José's face, hoping to see the same excitement I felt.

"E-ho-lay!" He gasped as the magazine slipped through his fingers and fell to the ground, opening to the centerfold. He kicked it closed with his foot and made the sign of the cross.

I climbed out of the car with the rest of the magazines and stood beside him, smiling. "Quite a find, huh?"

"This is disgusting," he said, nudging one with his foot.

"It's just a picture of a naked woman . . . and man," I said. "There's nothing wrong with the human body." That's what I used to tell myself when I looked at the magazines I hid in the backyard with my notebooks.

"This is a sin! Look at the way that man is touching that woman! That is a private thing . . . not something for somebody to look at!"

I glanced up, surprised at how angry he sounded. I'd never seen José so upset—even though I noticed that he couldn't keep his eyes off the cover of the picture at his feet. I looked at it too and felt a fluttering in my gut.

"Here," I said, embarrassed now and unsure of how José felt about me or how I felt about my reaction to the magazines. "I'll put them back. And I won't even look at them." I bent over and picked up the magazines.

"No," José said. "What if some little kid gets hold of them? What if they give somebody ideas and they try something on somebody . . . like my sisters or somebody?"

I swallowed. I hadn't thought of that. It was a scary thought. "Well, what should we do?"

"Burn them," he said.

So we scooped out a pit in the arroyo sand and piled the magazines inside. I didn't have matches, but José reached into the pocket of his jeans and pulled out a book of them. I was surprised. What was José doing with matches?

He saw the look on my face and must have guessed

what I was thinking. "I steal them from Arturo. A cigarette isn't any good without fire." He smiled.

And then we burned the magazines. As flames licked each page I imagined each of the curling, blackened people in the photos were burning in hell. It was a silly, childish idea, but I can't often control what goes on in my mind. We didn't say a word, and it took a long time because the magazines were thick and the paper was heavy and slick.

As the last page went up in flames, José looked up. "That's better," he said. I nodded and tried to smile. I would have enjoyed looking at those magazines—it would have been exciting. But I had to admit that, with the excitement, I'd always felt guilt and a little bit of shame. Maybe there was a good reason for those feelings. I had some thinking to do.

We covered the ashes with sand and walked slowly down the arroyo as if nothing had happened, letting our feet carry us where they would. The banks were getting low enough so that we could see beyond the arroyo.

And then José broke the silence.

"Did you practice with the piñones?"

"Yeah." I was relieved to shift my thinking to something else. "And I'm getting better."

José grinned. "You'll have to show me at school . . . on Monday." And then his grin melted. "How did it go with your mother?" he asked.

I'd been expecting that question, but I still hadn't worked out a good answer. "All right," I said, unsure of myself. I was still confused about my trip back to

Iowa. My mother and I had had some good laughs and some nice times. But I was still angry at the way she'd made telling her so difficult. And I was hurt and embarrassed about her reading my notebooks. I looked at José and saw him staring at me with big eyes.

"She didn't yell or get angry or try to talk you out of it?"

"Yeah, she did. But I'm here, aren't I?"

José turned to look out at the valley, nodding his head as he did. "Will she come out to visit?"

I wondered that too, even though she had promised to. "I don't know," I said. "I hope so."

"Me too."

I felt a cool breeze brush the back of my neck and turned around to look at the Sangre de Cristos. Some dark, threatening clouds had snuck up behind us. It often rained at this time in the afternoon.

"Want to visit your dad?" José asked.

I nodded and we began to trot, our elbows brushing against each other as we pumped our arms.

I ate until I was uncomfortable. Judging by the look on José's face he did too. But the food was so good, I couldn't help myself. I'd missed Florence's cooking.

Reluctantly José and I said good night to each other on the street in front of my house. I remembered that this was the same spot where I'd said good-bye to him before I went back to Iowa.

"Look at those stars!" I said under my breath, gazing at the night sky, not wanting him to go home—I sometimes wondered what it would be like to have José for a brother. The tail star of the Big Dipper shone brightly and I thought of my mother. I wondered what she was doing right now. Drinking probably.

"Yeah. Hey, I'm glad you came back. We're gonna have some fun, you and me."

"Yeah." I looked from the stars and grinned at him.

"See you tomorrow?"

"Yeah. Maybe we can go to the flea market."

"Yeah, maybe." And then he turned, hunch shouldered, and walked down the street. "*¡Buenas noches!*" he called over his shoulder. "Bro."

I walked back inside, feeling warm and happy from too much food and from José's parting word. Florence and my father looked up from where they sat on the couch, as if they had been waiting for me. Stopping, I grinned at them stupidly, wondering what was going on.

"Have a seat," my father said, waving his hand toward a chair in a formal kind of way. He cleared his throat. "I—we have something we'd like to tell you."

I'd expected my father and Florence to sit me down at some point and lay out the rules of the house—home by ten, no smoking or drinking, allowance, responsibilities around the house—all that kind of stuff. I'd been a guest all summer and had been spared that conversation. But now I was here for keeps and I wanted to pitch in and do my part. I wanted to know the rules.

I was not prepared for what came next.

"Son, Florence and I would like you to be the first to know." My father smiled at Florence and the two of them stared into each other's eyes for a long moment.

And then he turned back to me. "Florence and I are going to get married next week . . . during Fiesta."

Married? My face must have registered a dozen different emotions. I wanted to be happy, but my first reaction was fear. I was happy the way things were and I didn't want things to change. Before I could stop myself, I asked, "Why?"

Their faces froze. "I mean . . ." I felt stupid. "Why do you need to get married?" My mind struggled for words to explain the way I felt. "I mean, you're happy now, aren't you?"

I must have looked pretty funny, because Florence began chuckling, and then she began laughing. My father and I looked at her and then at each other, wondering what was going on.

"Well, now," she finally said. "I'm glad we didn't ask for *your* permission!"

I sat up straighter and I must have blushed. At least my face was burning.

"That's okay, Chester. I think I know what you're trying to say. Why get married?" She tipped her head to one side. "Because we'd like to announce our love for each other to our friends and to our families." She smiled at my father. "And to the world." She looked back at me. "It's like telling somebody you love them. Sometimes it's not enough just to love somebody. You have to tell them . . . out loud . . . often."

I felt like a creep. Still blushing, I got up from my chair and walked over to Florence. Bending down, I gave her a hug and kissed her cheek. It was soft as a new chamois cloth. I stepped over to my father and hesitated a moment. My father and I had never been much for hugging, so I held out my right hand.

"Congratulations," I said. He hesitated, took my hand, and then pulled me down to him. We hugged, the day-old stubble of his beard pricking the skin of my face.

NINE

▼▼▼▼▼▼▼▼▼▼

I don't often remember my dreams. But when I do, they're mostly the bad ones. The first week of school I dreamed so hard that I woke up tired every morning. And most of the dreams were terrifying.

At first I thought that maybe I was dreaming so much because I was worked up and nervous about most everything that was happening to me. I didn't know anybody in my school except José, and then there was the wedding. Plus, José was excited about Fiesta, and even though I didn't know very much about it, his enthusiasm for what was going to happen this weekend made me excited.

But after a couple of nights I saw a pattern. One particular dream happened every night, and every night it woke me up.

It would start nice and relaxed. I don't know exactly where I was in this dream, but I remembered soft music in the background, and light—soothing bright light that seemed to pour out of the sky like some kind of syrup. I would be sitting in a wonderful chair that really wasn't a chair because I don't think I was sitting on anything at all. But there I would be, sitting on a patch of firm air, relaxed and enjoying the feel of the light and the sounds of the music. And then my mother would appear, smiling and happy and beautiful.

She would reach out a hand and pull me to my feet from whatever I was sitting on and the music would grow louder and we would start to dance—a waltzing kind of dance, very old-fashioned and graceful. I've never danced in my life. But I remember thinking what a wonderful dancer my mother was and how nice it was to move to the music and to look up into her smiling face.

And then, slowly her smile would disappear. And then the music would get faster and louder—brassy and sharp. She began to hold my left hand so tightly that it hurt and she would pull me closer. Pretty soon I would find my face mashed against her shoulder and I wouldn't be able to breathe. And I wouldn't be able to hear the music so well because she was crying loudly. And I would feel her fingernails digging deeper and deeper into the small of my back where she held me with her left hand.

Finally, I would struggle for what seemed a very long time, shoving and pushing and clawing. My yells would sound like something coming out of several pillows pressed against my face. I would almost be suffocated when I finally pushed away from her and staggered a few steps backward. My mother's face would look horrid—all screwed up and wet from crying. And I would see that I had ripped parts of her dress when I struggled to get free. And then, while she was still crying, her eyes would pop open and she would begin to laugh. And then she would point.

I would look down to where she was pointing and I would see that I didn't have any clothes on. Nothing—except a shoe on one foot and a sock on the other. And I felt just the same as when she told me she'd read my notebooks.

Luckily, at that point, I would wake up.

It was a horrible dream. I would lie in bed for the longest time, furious with my mother, hating her for humiliating me in my dream. And then I would feel guilty and angry with myself for hating her. After all, it was just a dream—*my* dream—a dream *I'd* made up. It wasn't her fault that she did such horrible things in my dream.

Or was it?

It got so I didn't want to think about my mother, because that dream would pop into my head and then I would feel angry at her and then at myself. And I would miss her and love her and hate her all at the same time. Feeling all of those things at one time isn't easy, and I wasn't doing a very good job of it.

I was doing a much better job of getting ready for the wedding. José thought it was funny that I was going to be my father's best man. "I wish I could have been at my parents' wedding," he said as we walked home from school that Friday before the wedding. "Arturo was."

I frowned with my forehead and smiled at the same time. "Really?"

"Nobody says anything about it in our family, but all it takes is six fingers to count the months after they were married until he was born."

This was news to me. "They *had* to get married?"

"They were going to get married anyway." José grinned. We stopped in front of my driveway. "Like my grandmother says: 'When the tomato's ripe, pick it.' " He laughed. "Anyway, I can't imagine anybody except my mother being able to put up with my father. Hey, I'll come get you after dinner. Okay?"

I nodded. José was taking me to the first event of Fiesta—the burning of a giant statue called Zozobra—and he wanted to start early so that we would find a good place to sit.

I wished that my father and Florence had decided to have their wedding after Fiesta. But I understood why they were doing it now. Florence's art opening was the week after, and besides, the way they had it planned, it was going to seem as if the whole city of Santa Fe was throwing a giant party for them.

The wedding was going to be at our house, and the table in the kitchen was already filling up with presents. My present was among the rest of them somewhere, bought with the fifty dollars they'd given me for decorating my room. It was a wedding pot, made at the San Ildefonso Pueblo. Even though it had only one chamber inside, it had two graceful openings and the handle arched between them—symbolic of two people joined by love—poetry made of clay instead of words. I was proud of this pot and also embarrassed that I'd bought it for them with the money they gave me.

My dad and Florence wanted to have one quiet evening by themselves before everything got crazy with the wedding. It worked out well that José and I were going to the burning of Zozobra. Dad, Florence, and I ate a dinner of leftovers in the living room, balancing our plates on our knees and dishing out food from plastic containers on the coffee table.

Now that Florence was going to be my stepmother, I wanted to know more about her family.

"You were born in Pennsylvania?" I asked, knowing the answer but wanting to get her started. I was hoping she'd talk about something I didn't already know.

She nodded, then smiled, knowing exactly what I was up to. "Scranton," she said. "Sometime after the Revolutionary War and before television was invented."

"I always liked older women," my father said before slipping another forkful of food into his mouth.

She smiled and was about to say something to my father when I jumped in, not wanting her to get sidetracked by my father's little joke. "What about your parents?"

"My father was a coal miner and my mother was a teacher," she said. "My mother's dead but my father's in a nursing home there. I wish he could have come, but his doctors think the high altitude here wouldn't be good for his heart. He has black lung, you know." I wished her father could come too, so that I could ask him what kind of child Florence had been. She had promised to take me with her when she went to visit him next.

"And you were an only child?" I asked, probing.

She shook her head. "I have a younger brother. But I'm afraid we don't get along too well."

I remembered several evenings before when Florence told my father that her brother had written to tell her that he couldn't come. That they hadn't given him enough warning. That the flights would be too expensive. That he couldn't just take off and leave at the drop of a hat. She'd been hurt and relieved at the same time.

"Why don't you get along?" I knew I was being nosy, but this was the question I'd wanted to sneak up to all along. I couldn't imagine somebody not liking Florence, and I didn't have a clue as to why her brother didn't like her.

Just then the telephone rang. My father and Florence exchanged glances, not moving. "Would you . . . ?" my father began, turning toward me.

"Sure," I said, setting my plate onto the coffee table and rushing to the kitchen.

"If it's for either of us, we're not in," my father called after me.

I picked up the phone. "Hello?"

"Hi, Chester."

It was my mother. All the feelings from that horrid

dream came back to me in a flash, sharp and clear, and I didn't know what to say.

"I was hoping that you'd answer the phone," she said. It wasn't really fair of me, but I was listening carefully, analyzing each word she spoke. I wanted to know if she'd been drinking or not. She sounded as if she had.

"Hi," I said. I was happy to hear her voice and at the same time overwhelmed by all those feelings that came from the dream. "How are you?"

"Fine. Fine. Chester, I just wanted to call and say hello. It's been a week since you left. And I miss you."

She was beginning to sound a little more drunk than before, as if her guard was slipping. I didn't know what to say, so I said, "I miss you too." And I did.

"Would you tell your father and Florence that my gift is in the mail? Would you?"

"Yes." I hated the way this conversation was going. It sounded stupid and trite, but I didn't know what else to say.

"I want them to be happy. I really do." There was a long pause and I pictured my mother taking a sip of something, probably Scotch. "And, Chester, I want you to remember that—that you're still my son, even if Florence is your new stepmother . . . the new woman in your life."

Just then Florence walked into the kitchen, plates in both hands. She looked at me quizzically on her way to the sink.

"I love you, Son." My mother sounded close to tears.

"I love you too."

"Don't forget our star . . . this Sunday . . . ten o'clock."

"I won't."

"Well, I better let you go. I've got a *million* things to catch up on." She was rallying, trying to sound perky, but she wasn't doing a very good job. "Bye-bye. And give my best to the bride and groom."

"I will."

And then she hung up.

Florence turned from the sink. "How is she?" Her voice was gentle.

"Fine."

"Chester," she said in that tone of voice that means something important is going to follow, "I want you to know that I love you very much, but I don't ever expect you to love me the way you love your mother. What we've got is special, Chester, but your mother will always be your mother."

Before I knew what was happening, my eyes filled with tears. *Why couldn't feelings be simple?* The place in my chest where my heart was supposed to be felt like a nest of snakes. *Why did my mother call and ruin the gentleness of the evening? How could my mother do such a selfish thing?*

And then José burst into the kitchen, his eyes wild with excitement.

"Come on, Chester. If we don't hurry we won't get a good spot."

I turned away from him, brushed the tears from my eyes, and prepared a smile before I faced him.

"Go on, go on," Florence said. "We'll talk later." She nodded knowingly.

My father had followed José into the kitchen. "Come home right after," he added. "Don't go down to the Plaza. It gets wild down there."

I didn't know if José had noticed what was going on in the kitchen before he came in. If he did, he wasn't going to say anything.

José and I ran down our street and turned onto another, bigger street. It felt good to run, as if I was running away from the feelings conjured up by my mother's telephone call. The closer we got to Fort Marcy Park, where Zozobra was to burn, the more people we ran into, headed our way. I wished that I were about half my size so that I could zip in and out between people the way I used to. I was too big for that now, and too uncoordinated, and I had a hard time keeping up with José.

"This way!" he shouted over his shoulder, dropping into a shallow arroyo that paralleled the road we were on. Running in the arroyo sand was like running in deep snow. But after a couple of minutes we veered to the left and scrambled up a steep slope to the spine of a ridge. Teetering a little, I stood catching my breath as I looked down.

A swarm of people was gathered in the football field below. And staring down on them was Zozobra, a two-story monster dressed in a white gown made of paper, his eyes red and angry. He was also called "Old Man Gloom" and the people in the field had come to see him burn. The cry "Burn him!" popped up from all over, like the flashbulbs of people taking his picture against the night sky. According to tradition, when he went up in flame and smoke, so did all the bad feelings and gloom of the past year. With his death came the freedom from guilt and bad feelings.

It was exciting to finally see Zozobra. José had been talking about him all week. He was a fearsome monster, hooked by the back of his neck to a tall metal pole. His face was from a nightmare. Even so, there was something pathetic about him. He was trapped, surrounded by people who wanted to see him burn. Burn him! Burn him! I chanted in my head.

My arms twitched as Zozobra's arms twitched, and then his arms began to move slowly up and down, the forefinger of each hand pointing at the crowd and flopping slightly. I held my breath as the crowd became still and quiet. I could see men jumping up and down in the shadows behind the giant monster, pulling ropes to make him move. The jumping people looked incredibly tiny compared with Zozobra.

The lights of the field suddenly went out and everything was plunged into darkness. And then, just as suddenly, light leapt up onto Zozobra, seeming to splash him like cold water, and a startling moan erupted from the cave of his mouth. I gasped, unaware that he was rigged for sound. In a flash Zozobra seemed to rear up, seemed to grow to twice his enormous size. I wouldn't have been surprised if he'd lurched off his platform, crushing people with each step.

The crowd cheered and Zozobra groaned and his arms

jerked spasmodically. His head pivoted back and forth and his eyes shone fiercely up to the ridge where we were now sitting and then back down to the crowd.

I heard myself shouting, along with the crowd, "Burn him! Burn him!" My throat was raw. I'd been shouting for much longer than I had realized. It was at this moment that I became aware of how angry I was. I saw how close I'd been to exploding from my bottled up feelings—feelings of frustration about having to choose between my parents and about the hard time my mother had given me—frustration with myself for being so confused and so angry. These feelings had been trapped, like Zozobra, and were about to ignite.

The whole scene was something out of a nightmare. In the dark, the hills around us looked like crumpled piles of dirty clothes. Zozobra grew more frantic and so did the crowd. I stole a glance at José. He was quietly staring at the scene below, hugging his arms to his chest, looking both fascinated and scared. He didn't seem to notice that I was yelling.

The chanting below us grew louder and more frenzied. "Burn him! Burn him!" The words echoed off the hills, colliding with each other, shattering and coming together in strange combinations. I shouted too, even though my throat was beginning to hurt badly.

And then a figure dressed all in red, and wearing a crown made of spikes, danced into the light. The crowd roared and the Fire Dancer pranced at the feet of Zozobra, looking small, lifting his arms in menacing gestures, poking the air in front of the crowd, taunting the crowd, teasing them, taunting Zozobra, teasing him.

And then suddenly the Fire Dancer was surrounded by smaller figures in flowing white sheets. They danced and twirled and Zozobra screamed and his mouth flopped open and snapped shut.

My heart was racing and even though the night was cool against my cheek, I was sweating. I took off my glasses and wiped the moisture off my nose so that they wouldn't slip down.

Zozobra's arms were now thrashing about wildly and smoke billowed from his mouth.

"Burn him! Burn him!"

Fire broke through the top of his head, creating an awesome crown of flames. The crowd hushed. Zozobra wailed. The Fire Dancer and the dancing ghosts paused and then disappeared into the shadows. The fire spread, licking at the giant's shoulders and moving quickly down his arms. Shrieks poured from Zozobra's mouth along with the smoke and his arms continued to jerk, a little slower now. And then bits of him began to slough off, flaming and smoky. His head turned and then stopped, tipping to one side and breaking away from his neck and landing where the Fire Dancer had been only moments before.

Zozobra was dead. And I was exhausted. He was dead and I was suddenly relieved and my anger was replaced by an incredible feeling of sadness.

The lights of the field below flashed on, and José and I scrambled back down the slope and into the arroyo. I felt lighter, physically lighter, and for the first time in weeks I began to relax inside—to feel less tense.

▼

But the sadness remained, as if to anchor me to the ground.

Looking back on it, I have a hard time separating the wedding from the Fiesta—the parades from the parties, the ceremonies from the parades.

The wedding was like a dream. The music was provided by a string quartet whose members were friends of my father and Florence. The music they played was interesting but seemed to be made up of notes that came from between the cracks in a piano keyboard.

Florence looked lovely in a flowing gown the color of apricots. And my father looked dapper in his favorite tweed. The bolo tie that he wore was his wedding gift from Florence—a large sand-cast silver design with a large chunk of turquoise in the middle. The bridesmaids were dressed in matching skirts of stone-washed denim. I wore a blue blazer and gray flannel pants and a tie whose color reminded me of a dog's hanging tongue on a hot day.

As the best man my main job was to give my father the wedding ring. I kept my eyes on the minister, and when the time came, I handed it over. All I remember about the party that followed was that it was lively. At least I was lively. I'm never going to drink champagne again—it sneaks up on you. José and I didn't think we'd had enough to get tipsy, and then it hit before we could do anything about it.

Sunday started out slowly and continued to get slower. There was a disorganized parade to watch. Fiesta had been going on since Friday night, and people around town were beginning to look worn out. Bottles and litter covered the Plaza and filled the gutters of the streets that radiated from it like the spokes of a wrecked wagon wheel.

The last event of Fiesta is a candlelight procession from the Cathedral to a large white cross on top of the Hill of the Martyrs. José's family always goes to Mass in the Cathedral and then joins in the procession. He invited me along, but not being Catholic, I felt funny about going. Besides, I wanted to be alone. And I didn't want to miss talking to my mother through our star.

After dinner when I stepped outside and looked at the sky, I was disappointed to see a layer of high clouds had moved in during the evening. There wasn't a single star in the sky. It was as if I could suddenly see the barrier that kept me from telling my mother what I was feeling. I walked around the back of the carport, up the trail to the top of the hill, and looked out over the city. I tried to imagine the stars above the clouds, shining away. I thought of talking to her anyway. After all, the tail star of the Big Dipper was still up there, even if I didn't know exactly where it was in the sky.

And then, out of the corner of my eye, I saw a growing puddle of flickering lights by the Cathedral.

Stars! It looked as if the stars in the sky were gathering in Santa Fe on this cloudy night. I liked this fantasy. As I watched, the lights stretched out into a thread that bent one way, went in a straight line, and then bent again.

I hadn't realized that I could see the candlelight

procession from this hill. José had described it to me and I watched it with increasing interest, listening for hymns sung in Spanish. I was too far away. Looking beyond the Cathedral, I searched for the large white cross that sits atop the Hill of the Martyrs. I saw it, lit from below with a ring of floodlights.

The string of lights crept toward this cross, occasionally disappearing behind buildings or hills. From where I sat, I couldn't see the trail that winds up the hill. But I saw the lights collecting in a growing pool on the hill's top, surrounding the white cross.

The lights flickered for ten or fifteen minutes and then, one by one, they went out. I sat in the dark for a long time, seeing these starlike specks of light in my mind.

The Fiesta de Santa Fe was over and I was very, very tired.

TEN

▼▼▼▼▼▼▼▼▼▼▼

There were lots of kids missing from school the next day, and those of us who were there didn't especially want to be. At least I didn't. Everybody seemed sluggish and dreamy, including the teachers, who gave us little busywork assignments so that the absent students wouldn't miss out on too much.

José wasn't at school, which made me realize how much I'd been relying on him the past week. We had only one class together, but José knew lots of people and he'd been wonderful about introducing me to them, telling me who to avoid and who to be polite with and coaching me on the kinds of things to talk about—especially things not to talk about. School was different without him.

I wasn't the only Anglo kid in school—the school was about half Hispanic and half Anglo—but I felt as if I stood out, as if there were subtle rules of behaving that I wasn't aware of. Even the Anglos talked with softened Spanish accents. I would have felt foolish trying to sound like that. It just wasn't me. It would have been like trying to sign my name with my left hand.

But I decided that day that I would have to learn Spanish to get around—at least enough to understand the Spanish phrases I heard that sounded cool or vaguely obscene or insulting. I thought José would be a good teacher.

The day dragged. By the time I got home I was exhausted, and it was disappointing to lie down in bed and not be able to fall asleep.

I took off my glasses and closed my eyes, determined to take a nap before I went to see if José was really sick or just tired from Fiesta. As my arms and legs relaxed, 1 imagined myself floating in the sky, my head cradled by a pillow of clouds. Imagining this created in me a strange combination of soothing and scary feelings. It almost worked—I was just about to fall asleep when I imagined myself slipping through the cloud, grabbing for misty tufts as I fell, tumbling with nothing between me and the earth but air.

I sat up with a start, put on my glasses, and looked out my window into the side yard, with its neglected raised flower beds. It was such a different view than from my bedroom in Iowa. Everything seemed to hold everything else together—lumpy river rocks held the flowers together and the flowers held the rocks together. Without each other the whole arrangement would have collapsed into a heap of rubble.

The week before, I'd gotten stronger lenses for my glasses. Before I got them, I hadn't been aware that the windows in my bedroom had screens on them unless I was right up close. With my new lenses I could see all kinds of cluttery details that I hadn't been able to see before and that I didn't especially want to see.

I've often thought that looking through window screens gives outside views the texture of oil paintings—the wire grid becomes the warp and weave of stretched canvas. What I was looking at from my bed would make a pretty painting—it was well framed, illuminated with the long light of the late afternoon. There was a touch of fall in the light that deepened the colors of the honeysuckle vines, vines that groped and twisted against the stone wall above the flower bed. Fewer hummingbirds than last week zipped in and out of the picture to drink at the fluted flowers. They were migrating south. But when two or more arrived at one time, they often fought over the same bunch of flowers. One hummingbird in particular was a bully, charging the others at full speed. It was a wonder that he didn't skewer one of them with his needlelike beak.

I was enjoying this show when I noticed a shadow creeping across the grass, toward the honeysuckle. I sat up higher in bed and watched Tuxedo Cat creep closer to where the hummingbirds were feeding. Hummingbirds are nimble, flying so fast that they become blurs, and I thought the cat was crazy to think it could ever catch one. I didn't think it was possible.

Tuxedo Cat sat for a few minutes, hunched, its tail barely flicking. The birds seemed either not to see the cat or not to be concerned. I wasn't worried, especially when Tuxedo Cat slowly turned around to face away from the honeysuckle, toward my window. The cat sat, its ears cocked slightly backward, and closed its eyes. It looked as if it had gone to sleep.

Hummingbirds came and went, flying into and out of the picture, and the cat sat, not moving. I was certain that the cat was asleep, because several times a hummingbird flew right over it and the cat didn't even twitch a whisker each time this happened.

And then, without even opening its eyes, Tuxedo Cat leapt straight up just as a bird flew overhead. Relaxed and graceful, the cat landed on all four feet, and to my horror I saw wing feathers sticking out of its mouth as it trotted out of view.

I jumped out of bed and rushed through the house to the front door. Now I realized what the cat had been doing. It had been listening to the sounds of the hummingbirds and had calculated just the right moment to leap into the air to nab one from behind so that the little bird didn't see what was happening and swerve out of the way.

Although I ran as fast as I could, I didn't run fast enough. As I rushed into the front yard all I saw was Tuxedo Cat's tail, held high, disappearing around the stone wall and into the neighbor's yard.

I felt like going back to the side yard and pulling all the flowers off the honeysuckle. I wondered how many times those flowers had lured birds into the yard and then into Tuxedo Cat's mouth and stomach. *Stupid cat! Stupid flowers!* I raged in my head.

When I got into the side yard, I saw three hummingbirds hovering around the honeysuckle, unconcerned and jockeying for position around the flowers. "Git! Git!" I shouted, running toward them and waving my arms. "Go on! Don't you know any better? Get out of here!"

The hummingbirds scattered and I stood in the side yard, winded, feeling that the whole thing—the flowers, the birds, and the cat—were an awful, cruel setup. Scaring the birds had felt good. But I knew that they'd come back and that Tuxedo Cat would come back. I wondered how many hummingbirds Tuxedo Cat had eaten over the summer. Over his lifetime.

It depressed me to realize that I could stand there until I died but that hummingbirds would just go to some other flower and, right behind, would be Tuxedo Cat or another wily cat and it would all be the same. It depressed me to realize that there was no way in the world I could protect all the hummingbirds in the world from all the Tuxedo Cats in the world. But if they were going to get caught and eaten, I just didn't want to *see* it.

Keyed up and frustrated, I headed for the hill behind our house. As I passed Florence's studio I saw her sitting next to the window and staring out. I must have startled her, but she recovered quickly and beckoned for me to come inside and join her.

I walked into her studio, into the smell of turpentine and oil paints, and sat in an old, worn-out, overstuffed chair that Florence had thrown a yellow sheet over. Springs groaned and the tip of my rear felt the floor just as I stopped sinking.

"Well, look what the cat dragged in," Florence said, looking up and smiling.

"You saw." I stared at her.

She looked puzzled as she sat back on her high stool and laid her large sketching pad flat on her lap. "Saw what?"

I didn't know if she was teasing or not. If she was, I didn't think it was very funny. "The black-and-white cat catching a hummingbird."

Her eyebrows arched. "That cat caught a hummingbird?" I nodded and described how the cat had gone about catching a hummingbird by listening to the sound the bird made flying, not even opening its eyes to see where the bird was.

"Well." Her shoulders dropped as she rested her elbows on her sketching pad. "I wonder who that cat belongs to."

"It's a stray," I said. I'd asked José and he told me that he thought the cat lived under the trunk of a fallen-down apricot tree in a neighbor's backyard.

Florence thought about that for a moment. "Maybe if we fed it, then it wouldn't catch hummingbirds. Maybe we could make it fat . . . and lazy."

Her idea made sense. If the cat was a stray it was probably hungry most of the time. "Do you think it will work?"

"I don't see why not. I'll get some cat food the next time I'm at the store and we can see what happens." She picked up her sketching pad and leaned it outward from the tops of her knees. I thought that gesture was a signal that she had to get back to work and that I should leave. I was about to push myself up from the bottomless pit of the chair when she asked, "How was school today?" Then she reached for a piece of charcoal and looked at me over the top of the pad. Her arm made swooping motions and I heard scratching on the other side of the pad. She looked from the pad to me several times, finally stopping her sketching when I didn't answer and giving me a questioning look.

"I . . . well, it was kind of slow. A lot of people didn't show up today."

"Oh." Florence began sketching again. She squinted slightly when she looked down at the paper and opened them wider than usual when she looked up at me. I couldn't help noticing the shining gold band on the ring finger of her left hand. It looked good. "Too much partying over Fiesta, I suppose?"

I nodded, looking up from the ring to her face. "Even José wasn't there." I stuck my legs out in front of me as straight as they would go and sank further into the chair.

"Too much champagne." Florence craned her neck and stuck her face around the edge of the pad. She stared at me for a moment, smiled, and retreated behind the paper. "I hope you learned your lesson," she said.

Florence stared at what she was working on, leaning it out farther from her knees so that it was almost flat, but not flat enough so that I could see it. I felt awkward being here while she worked, and I didn't like having her give me a polite little lecture about drinking. I knew I had to watch out for alcohol, especially because of the way both my parents drank.

I brought my feet in toward the chair and was about to lift myself out of it for a second time when Florence looked up at me again. "Do you like the school you're in?" she asked. "I bet it's a lot different from the school you went to back in Iowa." She started drawing again and I let my feet slide out from the chair. I sank back with a sigh.

It was certainly different from the school back in Clifton. More faces and eyes were brown and more hair was black. The way people talked was different. But the locker doors slammed the same and kids complained just as much about homework and the cafeteria food tasted just as bad. There was the same mix of smart kids and athletes and greasers and gigglers and cheerleaders and hand-holding couples and wimps and loudmouths and quiet kids—like me.

"It's pretty much the same," I said.

Florence nodded. "Kids are kids, huh?"

"Yeah." I thought about telling her how good I was getting at shelling and eating piñones in class. But I didn't know if she'd approve or not.

She flipped over a page in the pad, stared at me hard,

and continued sketching. Her elbow stuck out from the edge of the paper.

"Florence?" I grabbed the arms of the chair and leaned forward. "Are you drawing me?"

She glanced up and winked at me and continued drawing.

"Florence? Are you?"

"Yep." She stopped and lowered the pad so that I could see her whole face. "And I'd like for you to look out that window for a moment so that I can capture the side of your face."

I didn't know what else to do, so I looked out the window. "Would you mind lifting your chin a little?" she asked. "That's it."

I stared at the old ratty geraniums that sat in front of the window—the same ones that had attracted the hummingbird into the house the day before I went back to Iowa. Some dried-out blossoms stuck out from a handful of small, droopy leaves. Florence was forgetful about watering them.

"Would you mind looking the other way? And would you sit on the arm of the chair?" She turned to the next piece of paper. I tried, unsuccessfully, to catch what she'd sketched as the top piece flipped over.

I struggled out of the chair and sat on the arm, facing the way she told me to. "Would you rest your hand on your thigh?" she asked. "That's good."

I wasn't comfortable balanced on the chair. I wondered how long I could sit like that without falling over.

"Chester, I know this is going to sound strange. But

would you mind taking off your shirt for me? I think I've almost got what I need for that painting. But it would help me to see some real muscles." She nodded to the corner where her easel stood. The canvas faced away from me.

I don't know why I felt nervous about it, but I did. My fingers were stiff as I unbuttoned my shirt and took it off. My skin felt goosey and cooler than the air. I draped the shirt over the chair's back and sat on the chair's arm again. "Like this?"

"Perfect . . . almost," Florence said. "Just lean back a bit . . . that's it." She lowered the pad enough so that I could see her mouth as she worked. The tip of her tongue stuck out and her mouth was pursed and her nostrils were pinched as she concentrated.

I felt an itch develop somewhere near my right shoulder blade. I didn't know if I should scratch it or not. Florence looked up every few seconds or so, her eyes seeming to snatch different parts of me, fitting what she brought back onto the paper with her eyes, and then weighing it down with the charcoal. But the itch continued to grow stronger and to spread. Finally, while she was looking at the paper, I reached up and swiped at the itch, raking my fingernails across my back. The itch shrank to a small point and then disappeared.

"There!" Florence laid the pad flat on her lap and sighed as she looked up at me. "Thanks. I was almost ready to give up for the day and then you walked by outside."

"Could I see?" I asked, grabbing my shirt and putting it on as quickly as I could. The buttons seemed to have grown twice as big as the holes. I walked over to her and looked down at the drawing.

I was on the page, all right. It was my head and my face and my shoulders and stomach. But it didn't stop there. There were my legs and my feet and my everything else. The boy in the picture was naked. First in my dream—and now this! First with my mother—and now with Florence! What was going on?

Florence saw the look in my face and began to chuckle. "Now, Chester. You know that's not really you. It's just a study for the painting I'm working on and I was just trying to get everything to fit together . . . get the proportions right . . . and the gestures right."

What amazed me was how real the part of me looked that hadn't had clothes on. I was pretty certain that Florence had never seen me naked before. Seeing myself that way in a picture made me think about the magazines in the arroyo—and the ones I used to have in Iowa.

"You're not upset, are you?" Florence was concerned. "Maybe I should have told you what I was trying to do."

The question came out before I had a chance to think about the best way to ask it. "Why is this kind of picture okay and other kinds of pictures of naked people aren't okay?"

Florence grunted and leaned back on her stool. I almost thought she'd fall over, but she didn't. "That's a tough one to answer, Chester." She looked at me for a

142
▼

moment and then out the window, past the geraniums. "The human body is beautiful . . . very beautiful. I think we grow up being ashamed of our bodies, and our bodies become strangers to us. That's tragic." She looked back at me and leaned forward, much to my relief. "I can't think of anything that is more graceful and more interesting and more beautiful than a human body . . . a man's or a woman's . . . a body that is completely naked and natural and comfortable with itself." She tipped her head to one side. "I think what you're asking is how this"—she motioned toward the sketch—"is different from pornography. Well, pornography isn't concerned with beauty. It . . ."

She looked back to the window and I did too, feeling embarrassed now that I'd asked—but wanting very much to hear her answer.

"I know!" Florence said in her operatic voice. "A hummingbird is a beautiful thing. Just think about it . . . those colors and the way it moves and the sound it makes and its delicate beak and the fan of its tail." She leaned toward me, almost falling off the stool frontward. "But not everybody looks at hummingbirds like that. That black-and-white cat doesn't. All it sees is food and sport . . . not necessarily in that order." She sat back. "Some people, the people who look at pornography and who make it, look at a human body and they think about sport and—and I guess it must feed some kind of hunger that gnaws away inside of them. But it's not like a cat's hunger. It's a sick and selfish kind of hunger. You see, they . . ."

She closed her mouth and looked at me. "Do you understand what I'm saying, Chester? Any of it? It's so hard to explain."

"I think I do." I wondered if I had that horrible kind of hunger gnawing away at me.

"A body is not just a sexual thing. In fact, most of the time it's not. There are so many other ways besides sex to appreciate our own bodies and other people's bodies. Sports, for example. Or dance. Or just sitting by a lake and feeling the breeze or seeing the breeze puff somebody's hair."

I knew she was right. But I knew I'd have to think about it some more. A lot more. When it came to thinking about girls' naked bodies, I had a clear and simple physical response.

Florence put her pad down. I must have looked bewildered, because she came over and leaned down and gave me a hug. "If I think of a better way to answer your question, I'll tell you. Go ahead and look at the other sketches I did of you while I get a snack for us."

I'm usually embarrassed to see pictures of myself, especially my face. But as I looked at the face that filled the page I flipped to, I have to admit that I was pleased by the way Florence had drawn me. She'd left off my glasses and made my eyes look . . . smart. And she'd made my mouth look as if I were about to smile . . . or was thinking about smiling. And the nose she'd drawn tied together the eyes and mouth beautifully. She'd left off my freckles and made my chin look the way I hoped it looked whenever I studied it in the mirror, turning it this way and that.

Florence walked into the room carrying a plate of cookies in one hand and a couple of cans of soda in the other. "I like them," I said. "Do I really look like that?" I asked hopefully.

"Yes, you do." Her eyes told me that she meant what she said, handing me a soda. "Would you pose for me again? I promise that in the future I'll draw you with your clothes on."

"Sure." As we sat in her studio, eating and chatting, I debated telling her about the dream I kept having about my mother. I almost did, but then I chickened out.

Looking back on it, I wish I had.

ELEVEN

▼▼▼▼▼▼▼▼▼▼▼

Lying on my back in the grass of the side yard, I closed my eyes and concentrated on sounds. The moment I closed my eyes, the sounds seemed to grow louder, as if a volume knob had been turned.

I heard the breeze rattling the yellowing, brown-rimmed fall leaves of the elm and cottonwood trees and the faint rumble of cars and trucks in the city. I heard birds and the quiet hum of insects as they doggedly worked the last remaining frost-burned flowers. I heard a flurry of shouts coming from the direction of José's house, but I couldn't understand what was being shouted. I heard the air whooshing through my nostrils as I took deep breaths, and I felt the gentle pulse of blood going through my ears and neck and arms and fingers. I wondered if, without meaning to, I timed my breathing to match the rhythm of my heart. Of course, the moment I thought of that I couldn't trust myself to breathe naturally so that I could tell.

As I listened, I realized that I would be hearing these very same sounds if I were in the backyard of my mother's house in Clifton. I found that I could form images of Clifton in my mind to match these sounds. A wave of homesickness washed over me. Sometimes I missed Iowa, terribly. I loved Santa Fe. But sometimes I felt as if I couldn't relax here, that I would always be a guest here, that I would never truly belong.

I missed Clifton, thinking about that day I'd spent walking around the town where I'd grown up, saying good-bye. I missed my mother, wondering how she was doing. I missed the cozy feeling of green closing in from every direction. And I missed cloudy days and drizzle and gray sky.

As I was lying there, feeling homesick, I heard the unmistakable rumble of Tuxedo Cat growing louder. I pictured him approaching the top of my head, his tail erect with just the tip flipped over, his ears cocked forward, slightly cross-eyed as he focused on me. Even his whiskers would be pulled back, as if blown flat by a wind.

The purring finally stopped and Tuxedo Cat sniffed at my hair, disturbing a few strands just enough for me to feel. I tried to remain perfectly still, not smiling, barely breathing. And then a soft heaviness landed on my chest. My eyes sprang open and I found myself staring into the half-closed green eyes of Tuxedo Cat, who had turned around to face me and was taking delicate little sniffs in the direction of my nose and mouth. And then suddenly Tuxedo Cat yawned—so wide, I could see over his pink and curled tongue to the back of his tiny throat. He was so close that I could smell his breath.

Hummingbirds?

I didn't know if the cat food was helping the hummingbird population or not. I suspected that it didn't make any difference, that a hummingbird was not much of a meal anyway and that Tuxedo Cat caught them for the sport as much as for food. But I do know that the cat food had made Tuxedo Cat plump. He spent most of his time in our yard and even wandered into and out of our house. In Florence's studio he had a favorite chair to nap in when the sun fell onto it, and he enjoyed our company when we were in the yard. Even though it was getting colder at night, we took a screen off the laundry-room window and left it partway open for Tuxedo Cat's safety. I didn't know if he slept inside at night. I suspected that he used it more for sleeping during the day.

The moment he saw my eyes open, he started kneading my chest with his claws and purring again. I lifted my arm and stroked his head, flattening his ears back with each stroke. He closed his eyes and reached out his chin, asking to be scratched there.

I'd never been allowed to have a pet in Iowa. And I really didn't even have a pet now. Tuxedo Cat didn't belong to me—or to anyone else that I knew of. I suspected that we were his pets more than anything else. But even so, I'd grown fond of him and was pleased every time he came calling. His life seemed carefree and just to his liking. I often wished that my life could be more like this cat's, that I could be perfectly happy with food, attention, and napping.

I was thinking these thoughts, and enjoying the satisfied look on Tuxedo Cat's face, when he suddenly dug his claws into me, tensed, and sprang over my head and into some nearby lilac bushes.

"Hi." I heard José's voice behind me. "How's it going?"

I sat up and turned around, rubbing my chest through my shirt, certain that there were eight little puncture wounds oozing eight little drops of blood where Tuxedo Cat's claws had nailed me. I pushed up my glasses with my other hand and saw that José was carrying the math text from school. And a notebook.

"I'm fine," I said, studying José. He didn't look happy. "What's that for?" I asked, glancing at the books.

"Well, I don't understand something," he said. "I asked Arturo to help me, but I still didn't get it right and he started telling me I was stupid, so I told him he was a pig." I remembered the yelling that had come from the direction of his house. "I don't think he knew how to do them either, but he didn't want to admit it."

"Oh." I frowned. "He called you stupid?"

"Yeah. Well, I was making him feel stupid because he couldn't explain it to me and he was making me feel stupid too. So I yelled at him and he yelled at me." He dropped down beside me. Lying on his stomach, he opened his textbook.

"What don't you understand?"

"Everything," he said, flipping through his notebook, trying to find the right page.

"Hey, wait a minute!" I stuck my hand between two pieces of paper and pushed the notebook flat. Covering the entire page were sketches of people's heads. They were so good, I knew who each person was.

I looked up at José and could tell that he was both pleased and embarrassed that I'd found these sketches. "You did these?"

He nodded. "When I'm bored or don't understand the teacher . . ." His voice drifted off.

"These are great!" I pointed to the one at the top of the page. "That's Geraldine Rivera. She's in your math class?" He nodded. "And that's Paul Facto," I said, pointing.

"Yeah."

Right below Paul's face was mine, with glasses and freckles and everything. "Hey, I'm not in your class!"

"I drew that from memory," he said. "Look. I didn't get your nose right."

It looked all right to me. Who looks at people's noses anyway? I mean, *really* looks at them. The harder you stare at a person's nose, the funnier it looks.

"You're good. I mean, you're *great*! Florence should see these."

"Come on," he said, embarrassed. "They're just stupid drawings. Show me how to do these problems."

I'm not the world's greatest student, but I am pretty good at math. My mother used to tell me it would come in handy someday when I took over the businesses. It was nice to be good at something, but the thing I wanted to be good in was the thing I got mediocre grades in. I wanted to be a writer, but so far none of my English teachers had noticed my obvious talent for writing.

"I'll help you if you teach me some Spanish."

José considered this for a moment. "Okay."

"And if you show these drawings to Florence."

He didn't say yes. But he didn't say no, so I helped him with his math. It wasn't too hard. I only got frustrated once when I was sure he wasn't listening to what I said—when he kept doing it wrong.

When we were finished, José got up. "You're eating at our house tonight, aren't you?"

I nodded. Tonight was Florence's gallery opening, and both she and my father were at the gallery making sure everything was hanging correctly and finishing last-minute, nervous things.

"Well, Arturo said he would drive us over there in his low-rider. But only if we're ready by the time he wants to go. He and Alicia want to go dancing tonight." He twitched his hips and smiled.

I love the smell of José's house. There's always coffee on the stove and a rich greasy smell from warming tortillas on an ancient iron griddle or from making sopaipillas in boiling oil. Grease seems to be part of the air, making it smooth—you could get fat just breathing the air—and it gets caught in your clothes so that you carry it with you when you leave the kitchen. And there is always a smell of beans and chili that never seems to go away, even when they have hamburgers.

At first I was afraid to go into José's house. His father is always scowling, even when he's in a good mood. And he doesn't speak. He shouts, even when he's not angry—it's just the way he talks. But José's mother is always pleased when I come over, and his grandmother is often sitting at the kitchen table napping or smiling—sometimes both at the same time.

"Help yourself at the stove," José's mother said as I walked into the kitchen. José was already at the table, beginning to eat. Next to him was his grandmother, balancing a cup of coffee in the palm of one hand, as if her palm were the saucer.

Arturo looked up from his food. "Here comes the great mathematician. Give him one bean and maybe he can multiply it into fifty and then divide it so we can all have some."

"E-e-e-e! That was a good one, bro!" José grinned at Arturo.

José's father growled. "And how many beans have gone into that car of yours?" He leaned back in his chair.

"That's enough talk like that," José's mother said, standing behind her husband and putting her hands on each of his shoulders. "I remember a car you used to have when we were young. I sometimes thought you loved it more than you loved me."

José's father smiled. "But I married you, not that car, eh?"

José's mother smiled back at him. "You took pride in that car, I remember. And it was a beautiful car too."

She looked around the table. "Does everybody have enough to eat?"

I wanted to ask what had happened to José's father's low-rider, but I was chicken.

José's grandmother smiled at me and I smiled back. She's almost deaf and her eyes are clouded, but I could tell that she'd seen my smile and that she was pleased.

It happened the same way every time. José's mother never sat down to eat until everybody else was served.

Arturo grunted. "Wait until you see the paint job. I'm going to put down twelve coats of paint," he said, looking at his father. "And it will have flames painted on the front fenders."

José's father laughed. "It will be a fine car, Arturo, of that I'm sure. A beautiful car. But it won't take you to college if you don't get better grades."

Arturo frowned. "Yeah. Sure." And then he turned to José and me. "I'll see you outside, pronto. Okay?" He left his plate on the table and went out the back door.

"That boy." José's mother sighed, getting up and taking Arturo's plate to the sink. "Just like his father. If Alicia can put up with him, she can have him."

José and I ate as fast as we could and then rushed outside.

The Red Devil's hood was up and I saw the white, grinning shape of Arturo's underwear sticking up from his sagging jeans as he bent over the engine. He was muttering sharp-sounding words, oaths that I couldn't quite understand.

José poked me in the ribs with his elbow and put his finger to his lips. Quietly we tiptoed back around the house, and as we hurried down the driveway José burst out laughing.

"E-e-e-e! That Arturo couldn't move that car with dynamite!" He laughed so hard that his arms and legs got droopy and he had trouble walking. He tried to imitate his brother's voice. "If you hurry I will drive you and Chester to the art opening." And then in his own voice José turned to me and said, "I want to get to the opening today . . . not next year!"

It would have taken us about as much time to drive as to walk. After a few minutes we came in sight of the gallery—a low adobe building huddling in the middle of a block of other low adobe buildings. There was a crowd outside, in the street, standing around, holding squat plastic cups in their hands, talking. I was relieved. I'd been worried that nobody would show up for Florence's opening.

It was an interesting group of people. One woman wore a white body stocking, white high heels, a white cape and hat, and tons of silver bracelets. The man who was listening to her talk wore leather pants and a gauzy white shirt that you could see tattoos through. And his nipples too. It was an impressive shirt except for that.

We made our way through these people to the door. When we got inside I searched for Florence and my father. I turned toward the sound of Florence's laugh and saw them in the far corner of the room, hemmed in by a half dozen or so people who all seemed to be talking at once. My father looked almost angry, but when he saw us, his face broke into a smile and he excused himself. Florence looked panicked for a moment, recovered enough to wave when she saw us, and continued listening and nodding her head all around.

"If you'd come a minute later I would have gone crazy," my father said, walking up to us and taking each of us in an arm and marching us toward a table that was crowded with bottles and cups and little open-faced sandwiches. "If I'd had to talk to those people one more minute, I would have strangled one of them."

Instead of waiting our turn, my father whisked us to the back of the table. The bartender gave us a weary smile and said, "Help yourself, Harvey." As my father poured three sodas, I looked at the people on the other side of the table looking at us. I noticed one shabbily dressed young man reaching around people and snatching sandwiches as he waited for his drink. He put more of them into his pocket than into his mouth. Other people must have noticed this, but nobody seemed to mind.

When we had our sodas, my father walked us over to a wall that had several paintings hanging on it with lights on a track in the ceiling aimed at them. A man and a woman were standing in front of one.

"This painting speaks to the child in me," the woman said. "Look at the corner, that upper right-hand corner, where that bird is."

"Yes." The man nodded. "And I love all the shades of blue. Makes it almost look like water instead of sky."

The man and the woman moved on to the next wall.

"What were they saying?" José whispered.

"I don't know," I answered.

"Neither do I," my father said. "What do *you* think of the painting?"

"It's beautiful." José spoke in a hushed voice. "I wish I could do that."

As I looked at the painting, I felt drawn to the bird. For a moment I almost felt that I was the bird, trapped for just a moment in the corner of the painting.

"Could you make that same feeling in words?"

I looked up and saw that my father had asked this question of me.

"I don't know." I looked back to the painting. "I could try."

He nodded, keeping his eyes on me.

I felt a hand on my shoulder, looked up, and saw Florence's weary face. "I'm glad you came." She looked up at my father. "Already five of them have sold!"

My father gave Florence a big hug and a kiss.

The opening lasted another half hour and then suddenly everybody disappeared, except for the lady who'd been dressed all in white. She walked over to Florence, clanking of bracelets, and gave her a peck on the cheek.

"You did *beautifully*," she said in a honey-smooth voice. "I hope you're pleased. We sold six more paintings since I talked with you last. That makes eleven altogether."

Florence was speechless. Her eyes were big and they were filling with tears.

"And I have a client from Pacific Palisades who would like you to do a painting for his living room. A com-

mission, dear!" This woman-in-white almost lost her
cool long enough to look excited. "You'll have to visit
his house to see the space he has in mind. At his ex-
pense, of course."

"Well," Florence said, finally, "I guess this means
we can fix up our car."

"Dear," the woman said, looking at Florence in all
seriousness, "this means you can go out and buy a new
one."

Just for a moment I wondered if my mother would
give Florence a deal on a new car. It was a nice thought,
but the moment it occurred to me I knew it was ridiculous.

Or was it?

Nobody said a word as we began walking home. Even
José was quiet.

"Hey, guess what?" I finally said, breaking the silence.

"Yes?" My father looked at me with that half smile
of his.

"José has some drawings that I think you ought to
see."

Florence looked at José. "Do you like to draw?" she
asked.

José nodded and gave me a look I'd never seen before. I didn't know if he was embarrassed or pleased
or angry or all three.

"Do you show your drawings to very many people?"
she asked.

"No. Just Chester," he said.

Florence nodded. "I'd love to see them, if you would like to show me. I know that when I was your age I was afraid to show anybody what I drew. I was afraid that they'd tell me it wasn't any good or that my flowers looked like trees."

José nodded, his face jumping to life. "I know. Arturo used to make fun of my drawings. He said that I made people look like walking sticks."

"Arturo's wrong," I said. "José's good."

"You know, I think a lot of people who have a talent are afraid of sharing it. It's . . ." She thought for a moment. "Having a talent is a little like having a dog's nose. You can smell things that people can't smell. And that's good and bad at the same time. You can smell things that are beautiful. But you also smell things that stink. And sometimes there are more things that stink than there are things that smell good."

"But there are so many beautiful things to see," José said.

"And lots of ugly things too," Florence said. "But having a talent like yours is special. You can see things other people can't. And you shouldn't ever let people tell you that you're not special."

José bent over and pretended to sniff the sidewalk. "Woof! Woof!" he barked, and then laughed.

PART IV

To pray is
To live
Is to pray.

CHESTER HORNIG

TWELVE

▼▼▼▼▼▼▼▼▼▼▼

"I can't believe it, but I'm hungry!" José's voice was loud as we walked out of the dim, waxy light of school and into the chromelike sunshine of the afternoon.

"Yuck! How could you be hungry!" My stomach shrank at the thought of food. Our last class of the day, the only one José and I had together, was biology and today we'd dissected eyeballs—real pig eyeballs, with shreds of fat still hanging on them. The smell of eyeballs still clung to the inside of my nose.

"What do you say we go to Tino's Grocery? He's got pickled pig's feet and fried pork rind." José stepped away from me in case I tried to punch him in the shoulder, and also to get a better view of my face. I didn't disappoint him: I screwed up my face until it felt like a wad of paper and made fake gagging sounds like paper ripping, starting at my throat and coming out my nose.

I pictured how the eyeball had sat on my desk, next to the razor blade I'd used to cut it up. It was facing up and its blue iris stared at me as if it could see. I'd turned it around, making it face the other way.

"Wasn't that neat, though?" José asked. "Didn't you think the eyeballs were neat?"

"Yeah."

"And how Mrs. Montoya got those eyes. E-e-e-e! I can't believe she did that!"

Before she passed out the eyeballs she told the class that she wanted each student to dissect his or her own eyeball—she didn't want any team stuff where one person did it all and the other person watched. So she'd gone to Art's Meat Market, where they slaughter their own pigs and cows and chickens and goats, and told Art that she needed a couple dozen pig eyeballs. She told us that he couldn't say no because he'd been a student of hers and he owed her a lifetime of favors.

Art, she said, had looked at her, wiping his hands on his bloodstained apron, and asked, "Well . . . do you want left ones or right ones?" And then, before she could answer, he'd asked, "Do you want blue ones or brown ones?"

She paused in her story to study us and to enjoy the looks on our faces. I didn't even know pigs had different-colored eyes—and I grew up in a state where there are more pigs than people.

She had smiled, her mouth creasing her plump cheeks

and making long dimples. "I told him that I wanted a couple dozen *mixed* eyeballs—like doughnuts."

Everybody in class groaned.

José shifted his schoolbooks from one arm to the other, waiting for an answer.

"Yeah, I think she did that," I said, picturing her walking out of Art's Meat Market with a grease-stained white doughnut-bag of eyeballs, each one staring in a different direction.

"Mine was hard to cut into. Was yours?" José asked.

"Yeah. Mine was *tough*." I'd tried to cut slowly, but I had to keep pressing harder and harder until my razor blade finally punched through. I remembered pulling the razor blade out of the white flesh as quickly as I could and being disgusted by the clear jellylike stuff that oozed from the cut. I had flashed on the image of jelly in a jelly doughnut squishing out when you take a bite. I have to admit that I'd gagged.

"And the optic nerve," José continued. "It stretched out, not as much as a rubber band, but it wouldn't break."

"The part I liked most was seeing how the lens fit into that place behind the iris."

"Yeah, and how the cornea was shaped. It was beautiful."

"I couldn't let the eye look at me while I was cutting it," I confessed, struggling to say what I'd felt. "I mean, it seemed as if I was looking at something that was looking back at me, as if I was looking into something that was *thinking* about what was happening and that

163
▼

it wanted to blink but couldn't blink because it didn't have any eyelids." I was describing it better than I thought I would. "It looked scared."

He nodded. "What do you look at when people talk to you? Do you look at their mouths or their eyes?"

I thought about this as we turned onto the street with my father's store. "I look at their eyes." I've always felt that eyes are windows to feelings and thoughts, that they don't hide or disguise fear or sadness or pain or happiness easily, the way the rest of the face can.

José nodded. "I look at mouths. Maybe that's why I didn't mind cutting up the eyes."

All this time I'd been communicating eye to eye. But now, looking at José, I didn't know what to do with my mouth. What was he seeing in the way it looked that I didn't know about? It made my mouth nervous.

I smiled anyway.

We walked into the bookstore. I was surprised to see that my father wasn't at the front counter with the cash register. José walked over to a display table by the front window and began leafing through one of the large coffee-table books on Georgia O'Keeffe, so I wandered to the back room, which was filled with children's books and a few used books.

My father was scrunched up and sitting at the small table and chair that was just the right size for kids. He was leaning over his knees and scribbling on a legal-sized pad of yellow paper.

"Hi, Dad."

He jumped, banging the table with his knees and almost flipping it over. "Hello!" His eyes were wide as he looked up at me. "You startled me!" he said, as if I hadn't noticed.

"Sorry," I said. "What are you doing?"

My father shrank back to his normal, relaxed size and then shrank some more in embarrassment. "Well, Florence is always telling me that I should write a novel, that I have enough ideas and that I look at things . . . at life like a writer. So"—he gestured to the pad, which was surrounded by scraps of paper—"I'm writing a novel."

I looked from my father to the papers, letting this news sink in.

"Hey, Mr. Hornig," José said, walking up behind me. "Do you have any books with eyeballs in them? I mean books that have parts of the body all cut up?"

"You mean a book on anatomy?" José nodded and my father pushed himself out of the little chair. "Yes. I think we have a *Gray's Anatomy* and maybe some other things too. Why?"

"We dissected eyeballs today in biology, and I was just curious to see it in a book," José said.

My father walked around me. "Most boys want to look at the parts that show the sexual organs."

"Yeah," José agreed. "But not us."

"No. Of course not." I heard teasing in my father's voice.

Their voices turned to murmurs as they walked farther into the front room. I stepped up to the table with all the papers on it. I didn't want to get too close, in case my father walked in. I didn't want to look as if I was reading his novel without permission. But the temptation was too great. Pushing my glasses up to the top of my nose, I craned my neck and peered at the top page. His handwriting was never easy to read and the scrawl I saw was especially bad. I struggled to read a couple of lines.

For the first time in his life he felt as if he could do what he wanted. If he'd been a musician, he would have played the soft parts of the music loudly and the loud parts softly, the fast parts slowly and the slow parts so fast that his fingers would barely be able to keep up.

I'd felt like that before. I guess my father had also felt like that. It would be impossible to describe a feeling if you'd never felt it before, just as it would be impossible to draw something if you didn't know what it looked like.

"Hey, Chester!" José called from the front room. "Come look at this! This book's got *everything!*"

I turned from the table and saw my father leaning against the doorway, gazing at me. He'd been there a minute or two.

"It's just a start," he said quietly, stepping toward me. "Someday maybe you'll want to read the whole thing . . . if it's good enough." He paused and looked at the paper on the table. "It's a lot of hard work. And I realize now how much I've always wanted to write. I just never had the courage . . . to share my thoughts and feelings." And then he looked up at me and smiled. "And it also makes me realize that it can take just as much work to write a bad novel as it does to write a good novel. I hope it's good . . . because I'm spilling my guts on that paper . . . and dissecting them."

I didn't know what to say.

"If you want to see guts, José's got the right book." He grinned.

I nodded and smiled, wondering what my father looked at when I was talking: my mouth or my eyes. I hoped it was my eyes. I knew my eyes were honest. I didn't know about my mouth.

José and I looked at anatomy books until my father closed up the store. We mostly looked at that section on eyeballs, but we sneaked in a few looks at the sex organs. They didn't look very sexy, all cut up in cross sections with red for muscles and blue for veins and white for fat. They didn't look anything like the magazines we'd found in the arroyo. But then, I was beginning to think those weren't too sexy either.

I was doing my homework when my father walked into my room. Florence was right behind him. They sat on my bed and I could tell by looking at their faces that something was wrong.

"Chester," my father began, "we just got a phone call." I remembered hearing the phone ring. But that had seemed a long time ago—maybe as much as a half hour. "It was about your mother. I'm afraid it's bad news."

I shook my head a little, trying to clear it of math problems. A chill crept over my skin, coming from inside of me, not from the air. It's strange, but looking back on it, I'm pretty sure I knew what was coming.

My father looked down at his hands, which were tangled and white at the knuckles. He pressed his mouth together and looked up at Florence, asking her with his eyes to continue.

Florence sat up straighter and took a deep breath. "Chester, your mother tried to kill herself last night. Luckily the maid . . . Bertha? . . . found her this morning. She's in the Clifton hospital and they think she's going to live, but she isn't awake yet."

My insides shifted, as if they were crumbling. My mother had tried to commit suicide? "How?" It was a strange question, but it was the first one to come to mind.

Florence squinted, not knowing what to think, and cleared her throat. "She took a handful of pills."

My father took one of Florence's hands in his. "The doctor thinks that the pills may have done some damage to her liver." He looked scared as he talked. "He thinks she's going to be all right, though."

I shuddered, picturing my mother in bed, her face a whitish gray, her eyes staring but not seeing. Dead. Like the pig eyes today in science. My stomach twisted.

"Why?" But I knew the answer even before I finished asking. She tried to kill herself because I'd left her—because I'd chosen my father instead of her—because I'd rejected her—because I'd been selfish—and because she needed me.

It was my fault.

"No!" I didn't mean to shout, but I did—loudly enough to startle myself. And then I began to cry.

Florence got up from the bed and walked over to

me, wrapping her arms around my shoulders. Before I could stop myself, I pushed her away. I tore off my glasses and flung them across the room—just as I used to do when I was a kid. I ran from my room and out of the house. Dusk was falling and everything was a blur, but I didn't want to see—I didn't want to see or feel or think. Blindly I scrambled up the trail to the top of the hill, gasping with the effort of trying not to cry, but crying anyway, not seeing anything, not feeling anything but the pain of knowing it was my fault.

When I reached the top, I stood gasping. Without my glasses I felt tipsy, as if the world was falling away from where I stood, into the night's darkness. My crying turned to hiccups. Finally my legs gave out and I sat. Dazed, looking around, I saw clearly only those things close to me. I'd just missed sitting on the little barrel cactus.

"Chester! Chester!" I heard Florence calling from below.

"Chester!" There was panic in my father's voice.

I didn't answer. A numb, stony anger had replaced the shock and hurt. If they hadn't talked me into coming back to Santa Fe, my mother wouldn't be in a hospital right now. She wouldn't have tried to kill herself.

It wasn't my fault alone. It was their fault too.

I sat for a long time on that hill, growing colder and colder as the rocks and dirt lost the heat they'd soaked up from the sun. Without my glasses I felt as if nothing existed outside myself, that everything outside myself was confusion. I closed my eyes to the bleary night lights of the city. The sky seemed like the iron lid of a skillet clamped down on top of me. I could almost feel it pressing, flattening the top of my head. I felt more alone than I'd ever felt before. I felt betrayed by Florence and my father. And I felt ashamed of myself for being selfish enough to leave my mother and live in Santa Fe.

Florence's voice floated up toward me again. "Chester! Chester!" It was higher than usual and I could tell she was scared. I hugged my knees to my chest and smashed my nose into the groove made where my thighs came together.

I couldn't stop blaming myself for what had happened to my mother. It was my fault. If I'd stayed in Clifton she wouldn't have tried to kill herself. The only way to protect myself from these thoughts was not to think—to keep my brain blank—to slow everything down.

One thought grew like a bubble: Life isn't supposed to be happy. When you're happy—the way I'd been in Santa Fe—something always happens and it hurts too much to go from being happy to being unhappy. It's better to be low-grade unhappy all the time—like a slight fever that makes you achy but not sick. It doesn't hurt as much when things go wrong, it's not that much of a change. That's how I'd been in Iowa. I decided that was how I was going to be from now on.

I knew what I had to do. I had to go back to Iowa. I had to go back to live with my mother. I had to take care of her, and when I grew up, I'd have to take over the car dealership, manage the farms, and sit in her seat on the bank's board of directors. Just like she'd said.

And then I heard José calling for me. His voice was growing louder. "Chester!" He was coming up the trail, climbing the hill.

I didn't want to see or talk to anybody. José was as much to blame for what my mother had done as anybody. He'd told me I shouldn't go back and I'd listened to him.

Lurching to my feet, I turned away from the trail and scrambled down the hill. Moving made me dizzy and queasy—everything was as blurred as if I'd been riding a Tilt-A-Whirl. I wished I hadn't left the house without my glasses. Dislodged rocks bounced ahead of me, making a racket. If I kept moving, I knew that José would hear me and then know where I was. So I just sat down, not bothering to find anything to hide behind, hoping that the dark would keep me safe if I hunched over and made myself small.

It worked. I heard José walking around above me. He called my name several times. And than I heard him leave, going down the other side of the hill, following the trail that led to the arroyo.

I perched on the side of that hill for a long time. I was getting used to not being able to see very well. Smells and sounds had become clearer. A moistness had crept into the air, filled with the scent of soil. And the sounds of the city had gradually died, coming and going in gentle waves—as if the city itself was muttering in its sleep.

As I sat on the hill, looking down on a quiet Santa

Fe blanketed in darkness, I thought about sleep. It occurred to me that sleep requires trust. If you didn't trust the fact that you'll wake up in the morning, you wouldn't be able to go to sleep. You'd lie awake all night in fear, waiting for the worst—unless, of course, you didn't want to wake up—like my mother.

She'd fallen asleep hoping that she'd never wake up. Or had she? I'd heard that some people who try to commit suicide don't really mean to kill themselves. I'd heard that these people go through the motions of killing themselves because they're crying out for help, trying to communicate with actions things they can't communicate with words.

Had my mother really meant to kill herself? It occurred to me that maybe she hadn't. I didn't know which devastated me more: my mother trying to kill herself for real or my mother going through the motions of killing herself to get attention.

My head was growing as sore as my rear. Feeling stiff, I stood and slowly picked my way to the bottom of the hill. Bushes brushed my feet off to the left or the right and rocks put a wobble in each step. I'd never gone down this flank of the hill before, so when I reached the bottom I was a little surprised to find myself in José's backyard.

The house was dark and everything in the backyard had an underwater appearance, sunk beneath inky pools of shadow. The black hulk of Arturo's car huddled inside the carport. I stared at it gloomily, thinking that I'd be back in Iowa before I got to ride in it.

I walked over to the car and ran my hand over the

roughness of its primer-coated fender. My hand continued down the length of the car and I followed it. I
stopped when my hand found the handle to the driver's door. Pressing my thumb down, I eased the door
open and slipped behind Arturo's new steering wheel.
It was small, no bigger around than a dinner plate, and
made from a ring of chromed chain that had been
welded together.

A wire poked up from the torn upholstery and I
shifted my weight so that I wasn't sitting on it. Running my hands around the smooth bumpiness of the
steering wheel, I wished that I could drive this car away,
that I could drive it anywhere—far away from Santa
Fe, far away from Clifton.

I closed my eyes and imagined myself driving down
a long stretch of road. It was night in my mind and I
pictured the moon shining down, making the road look
like a river. I imagined the car gliding as smoothly as
a boat—so smoothly and silently that I could have been
flying instead.

And then I was flying. The nose of the car pointed
up and was aimed for the moon. It banked sharply to
the right and my hands slipped off the steering wheel
and fell softly onto my lap. Banking more sharply, the
car turned, spiraling upward in wonderful loops. With
each loop I grew more relaxed, and leaning with the
spiral, I tipped over onto the length of the seat.

I must have fallen asleep, because that was how Arturo found me the next morning, curled up in a ball
on the front seat of his low-rider.

THIRTEEN

▼▼▼▼▼▼▼▼▼▼

I woke to the smell of cigarette smoke. My eyes flew open and I pushed myself up so that I was sitting, all the while frantically looking around, not knowing where I was. And then I saw Arturo's face, as unfocused as the man on the moon.

He sat in the driver's seat looking at me, one knee propped against the steering wheel. Slowly he raised his cigarette to his mouth, inhaled, and blew a stream of smoke toward me, which made his face disappear.

"I wondered how long it would take for you to wake up," he said, squinting at me, his vague face reappearing as the smoke thinned and cleared. The sun had not yet climbed over the tops of the hill behind us and his voice was as soft as the dim light.

"Hi," I said, pushing away from him. The armrest

of the passenger door jammed into the small of my back.

He put a finger to his lips, signaling for me to be quiet, and then took another drag of his cigarette. "Every morning I come out here and wake up the rooster and have my first smoke of the day," he said. "I like the quiet and having a few minutes to myself. Only, today I find you here, curled up like a sick dog." He flicked what was left of his cigarette out of his window and sighed. "You sleep here all night?"

"I—I guess so." Bits and pieces of last night were coming together in my mind, not quite in the right order but enough to bring back all the bad feelings.

"Want to tell me about it?" He sounded bored, but even without my glasses I could tell that his eyes were alert and watchful.

I didn't know what to say. My face felt as rumpled as slept-in sheets and I kept blinking, hoping that everything would come into focus. Without my glasses that was impossible. The only thing I could see clearly were my hands when I looked down at my lap, where they held on to each other like lost children.

"I heard about your mother," Arturo said. I looked up. "It's a hard thing, no? And when you're hurting bad, spread some of that hurt around. Make sure everybody gets a taste of your hurt. Did it make you feel better . . . to spread it around?"

I was a half step behind his sarcasm. But just as I understood what he'd said, and was going to protest, he began talking again. "José, he was worried sick about you. He looked and looked, everywhere. He went to bed last night thinking you were lost or gone or something. He was grieving, man. He was grieving for you." He pulled another cigarette out of his shirt pocket and stuck it into a corner of his mouth without lighting it.

"I didn't mean—"

"Look," he said, closing his eyes halfway, the cigarette wagging up and down as he continued talking. "I got to thinking last night after José told me all about it. I got to thinking that sometimes life slaps us around a little . . . you know, picks a fight with each of us. Some of us, when we get slapped around, we slap back. And some of us, when we get slapped around, we run away."

Was he calling me a coward? I dropped my head and stared at my hands. I didn't want him to see how much he'd just hurt me.

"Hey, Chester." I looked up, surprised by the sudden gentleness of his voice. "You a fighter or a runner? Huh?"

The back door of the house creaked open, followed by José's voice. "Hey, Arturo! Quit making love to your car and have some breakfast!"

Arturo sat up. "I'm coming!" he called over his shoulder. Taking the cigarette out of his mouth and putting it back into his shirt pocket, he turned to me. "Your mother, she tried running away from her problems and look what happened. Those problems just went looking for somebody else to pester. I think you better go home, Chester. You better stop running." He opened his door and got out.

Bending over, he poked his head inside the car and

grinned at me. "Come on, Chester. Don't run like a *cucaracha*. Get out and fight. Fight fair or fight dirty, I don't care. But fight." He boxed the air in front of him playfully and then his head disappeared.

He didn't close the car door when he left.

"Chester!" Florence sprang up from the sofa, and before I knew it I was in her arms. Her voice rang over my head. "Harvey, he's home. Chester's home!"

My father stumbled into the living room. He'd been sleeping and he didn't look fully awake. "Chester?" He stopped when he saw me and his eyes lit up. "Chester!" He rushed over to me and gave me a hug. "Where have you been?"

"Arturo's car."

He nodded, as if it was the most logical place for me to have been. "Oh," he said, taking my glasses out of his shirt pocket and handing them to me. I hesitated before putting them on. I was getting used to the world being softer and fuzzier. I put them on and found myself resenting the sharp lines crowding in on me.

Florence ushered me to the couch and sat me down. She knelt at my feet and looked into my eyes. I felt the couch shift as my father sat next to me. "I'm glad you're back," he said, putting an arm around my shoulders.

I braced myself for the scolding I expected—that I deserved. I avoided looking at them, instead looking over Florence's head, around the living room. I thought about how much I would miss this place—it felt more like home than the home I grew up in. This was a comfortable house, a house that slouched and made you feel okay about putting your feet up on the coffee table. It was so different from the house in Clifton. But I really had no choice. Not anymore.

Florence cleared her throat. *This is it,* I thought. "Chester, this has been a terrible blow for you, and I think I know how you feel." Her voice was calm.

I tensed. Why didn't she show a little anger? Why didn't she get the yelling over with? And how could she know how I felt?

She patted my knee. "Listen, I know you think that it's all your fault, that your mother tried to kill herself because you came here to live. But it's much more complicated than that. You shouldn't blame yourself. And you shouldn't think about going there to live . . . at least not until your mother gets better—gets the kind of help she needs."

I glared at her. Words my mother used came to mind and shot from my mouth. "It wasn't fair for me to make up my mind about where to live after spending the whole summer here."

Florence's eyebrows rose and then lowered, frowning. "The entire situation wasn't fair," she said. "I happen to think you made a wise choice. And I think what your mother just tried to do proves me right." She looked at me for a long moment, and I could tell she was thinking hard about what she was going to say next. "Do you think your mother tried to kill herself because you decided to live here?"

I stared back at her and refused to answer. It was an incredibly stupid question for her to ask. It was so obvious. *Of course that's why she did what she did! She didn't do it because she thought it would be fun!*

"She probably thinks that's why she tried to kill herself. And you probably think that's why. But, Chester, mothers don't do that if they are really and truly thinking about their children. Mothers don't do those things to children they love."

I grunted angrily at what Florence said. And then I shouted, "She loves me!"

"Of course she does." Florence tipped her head to one side. "I think she loves you . . . as much as she loves anything." She looked down at her hands and then up at me again. "I know when you two talked this summer, back in Iowa, she probably told you that we tried to make you think more of us by making you think less of her. It's only natural for a person to feel that way. I hope you know that's not true. We're not perfect. Nobody is. And I'm only telling you what I think is true. Then you have to decide if it's true for you."

I know she was trying to help. But she was making me more miserable.

"I believe people can only love other people as much as they love themselves. It's a tough thing to explain, Chester, and it's a tough thing to understand. It's taken me most of my life to understand. Look. If you were starving, you'd grab food out of my hand and stuff it into your mouth, wouldn't you? Even if *I* were starving, you'd take my food. I know *I* would . . . if *I* were starving. When you have enough food all the time, you're usually satisfied . . . content . . . you usually don't snatch food from other people and then eat it before they can get it back."

As she talked, I watched her face. It was the face of a person who liked food. It was a fat face, I thought meanly.

"It's the same with love. We need love as much as we need food. And some people are starved for love. They weren't loved as children so they don't love themselves . . . they grow up thinking that they aren't special or talented in some way or that they're not lovable. So these people . . . people like your mother . . . try to get the love they need from other people in any way they can. They will spend money so that people will love them. They will pester people into loving them. They will do *anything* to get people to love them . . . steal it, buy it, bully it."

I knew where Florence was headed, and I didn't like it—even though it was making sense.

She must have known what I was feeling. "Who knows why your mother tried to kill herself? Nobody except your mother really knows. But I have a strong feeling it was because she didn't love herself . . . because she was in such pain and was so empty and so lonely that she couldn't stand it anymore. Maybe she was just calling out for help. Maybe she felt that she'd already tried to get love every way she could think of and that none of it worked and so she finally gave up." Florence shrugged her shoulders and lifted her hands, palms up.

While Florence had been talking, I'd forgotten my father was sitting next to me until he pulled me closer to him. "Talk to us, Chester. Tell us what you're feeling. Don't run away from us." I'd never heard my father plead like that before. He sounded scared.

"It wasn't your fault," he continued, whispering into my ear. "It wasn't your fault. And it wasn't my fault either."

I began to shake. I didn't realize how much I'd needed his touch and those words. Why was everything so complicated? Why did people do these things? Why was life so rotten?

Why? Why? Why? Why?

I thought I'd cried about my mother on the hill. But that was nothing compared to the way I cried in my father's arms.

Before he went to the store, my father and I had a long talk. He told me things that I'd kinda-sorta known as I was growing up, but that I'd never really known for certain. I began to figure out why I'd hardly ever caused trouble, why I'd never really fought my mother when she gave away my clothes or overwhelmed me, making me do things I didn't want to do. I began to realize that, for as long as I could remember, I felt as if I shouldn't burden her with my bad feelings. I must have sensed how fragile my mother was, sensed that she had enough to deal with, that she might break if I gave her any more pressure.

My father told me that this was not the first time my mother had tried to commit suicide. When he told me this, I remembered several "trips" that she took to visit relatives that I'd never heard of before—or since—in places like Chicago and Minneapolis and even Des Moines. She always came back looking as if she'd fought a war—pale and thin and bruised around the eyes.

My father told me that whatever medication she was given to control her mood swings always turned vicious when she drank or took sleeping pills. He told me how much he used to blame himself for her fits of depression because he couldn't seem to keep alcohol and sleeping pills from her. It didn't matter how often he rid the house of them, she always found ways to get the booze and pills she craved.

He told me how he used to feel inadequate because he couldn't seem to make my mother happy. Sometimes he felt as if there was something terribly wrong with him. Other times he decided that my mother didn't love him enough, because it didn't matter how much time he spent with her or how many times he told her that he loved her, she would suddenly pull into herself and fall into an emotional cave that would take weeks for her to crawl out of.

It wasn't pleasant to hear these things about my mother. But knowing that my father had felt some of the same feelings, now made it easier for me to share my feelings with him. I'll always be his son and he'll always be my father. But that morning I think we began to be something else to each other. We became friends, people who would have chosen to be friends even if we weren't related to each other.

I slept most of the rest of the day, as if I was sick. I woke up to the late-afternoon light, disoriented and feeling brittle.

As I walked into the living room I heard voices coming from Florence's studio. One of them was José's.

"This is one of that arch at the start of our driveway," José was saying as I walked into the room. Florence and José were huddled around a table that she kept on one side of the room. Florence made a happy noise low in her throat.

"Look at the shadows!" Florence said. "And the tree. Look at the bark on the tree!"

I walked up to the table, surprising both of them.

"Chester!" Florence pushed back several strands of hair that had fallen into her eyes. "How are you?" She leaned over and gave me a hug. I was beginning to feel that, in this one day, I'd used up all the hugs I was allowed for the rest of my life.

I didn't know how I felt, but I said, "Fine."

José stood at the table, looking shy. "Hi," he said. His smile was uncertain. "You picked a bad day to miss school. We had a fire drill and we had a pep rally for the football team. The teachers gave up and we didn't do anything like they planned except . . ." He fell silent. "Hey, I'm sorry about your mother."

I shrugged. Talking and talking about my mother was beginning to feel like scratching a mosquito bite too much.

Florence pointed to the drawing on the table. "You were right, Chester. José has a lot of talent."

I looked at the drawing. The lines were confident and the arch appeared heavy and grand and the shadow made the top look just low enough so that a person would have to duck to go through.

Florence looked at me. "I was just talking to José about lessons. It's been a while since I've taught, but I thought it would be fun for both of us." She smiled. "It would be even more fun if you'd help us today."

"Sure," I said, wondering what I could do to help.

"Great!"

As Florence ushered me over to the chair in the corner I suddenly knew what she wanted me to do.

"I don't—"

"Don't worry," Florence said. "All you have to do is sit and look handsome."

José squinted at me. "I don't know if he's the right person for this job."

"I guess he'll have to do," Florence replied, playfully squeezing my shoulder.

It was a good day for being a model. I felt more like a thing—an empty thing—than a person. I sat, staring out the window, past the geraniums. Suddenly Tuxedo Cat swaggered across the lawn, his tail and head held high. And right behind the cat came a puppy dog I'd never seen before—a pup with floppy ears, its tail wagging so fast, it reminded me of hummingbird wings. The puppy stumbled, fell on its chin, quickly picked itself up, and hurried to catch up with Tuxedo Cat.

First the cat and then the puppy disappeared from my view. I hadn't seen such a strange thing for a long time. Where had the Tuxedo Cat picked up that puppy?

Where were they going? Why was the cat so calm? Why wasn't the puppy trying to play?

I began to laugh, surprising myself and Florence and José.

"Hey, quit moving," José complained, but I could tell he was glad to hear me laugh.

"What's so funny?" Florence asked, tipping her head to one side.

I shrugged, no longer laughing but unable to stop smiling. They wouldn't have believed me if I told them.

"This drawing's going to be weird if he doesn't sit still," José threatened.

A few minutes later, when José and Florence had finished, the three of us gathered around the table to see what they'd drawn. José's picture showed me smiling. Florence's showed me frowning. Florence's drawing had fewer lines and stronger shadows. But I liked José's better.

FOURTEEN

▼▼▼▼▼▼▼▼▼▼▼

The letter came several days later, and it took us all by surprise.

The day the letter came, I was in the kitchen talking with Florence while she made dinner, when my father came home. He looked grim as he lowered himself into a chair at the table. Usually he says hello and hugs whoever is handy. That day, however, he was silent.

"What happened?" Florence asked, drying her hands on a tea towel and walking up to him.

He reached into his jacket pocket, pulled out a letter, and held it out in my direction. "I thought about opening this . . . to see what's inside," he said. "But I think there's something wrong with opening somebody else's mail."

Puzzled, I took the letter and studied it. It had my

name on it. And the writing on the envelope was my mother's.

"How—"

My father interrupted. "I don't know what's inside. But the postmark is the day after she tried to kill herself, the day she was in a coma . . . in the hospital. I have a feeling that she stuck this in the mail the same day she took all the pills . . . that this might be a—a suicide note or a note to explain to you what she was about to do. I don't know." He sat back in his chair and sighed.

I sensed that what I held in my hands was a dangerous thing.

"If I were you, I don't know if I'd open it or burn it. I don't know *what* I'd do. When she's better she may wish she'd never sent it. She might wish that you'd never read it. At the same time she might have said some things that are important for you to hear . . . things she'd have a hard time saying to your face." He stared at me, his eyes tired and droopy. "I don't know what you should do."

Florence shook her head. "Incredible," she said, sitting opposite my father at the table.

I stared at the letter. If my mother had really meant to kill herself, she was expecting me to get this after she died. Maybe even after the funeral, after I'd come back from Iowa. Now that she was alive, she might have second thoughts about what she had written—if she remembered writing the letter at all.

I didn't know what to do. More than anything I wanted to be alone. I didn't know what I was feeling—

too much was going on in my head. I jammed the letter into the back pocket of my jeans.

"I think I'll go . . . for a walk."

Florence nodded as she heaved herself up to her feet.

"Dinner will be ready before too long. Should I call for you?" She must have known where I was going to go, that I would be able to hear her from there. I nodded.

I was about to turn to leave, when Florence stepped up to me. She wrapped her arms around me and held me. Before she let me go, she spoke gently into my ear. "Chester, we love you. And I'm so sorry."

I nodded. "I love you." I spoke under my breath, but I'm certain she heard me.

Santa Fe sprawled at my feet, darkening as the sun sank over the Jemez Mountains. Its streets were a jumble, looking like a tangled string dropped to the floor, forgotten in the rush to open a package. My thoughts and my feelings were jumbled in that way, seeming like streets that wrapped around and crossed over themselves, never going anyplace except back to where they'd started.

I longed for the east-west, north-south grid of Clifton. I longed for the direct route and for simple feelings. I longed for that and yet I remembered how trapped I'd felt in Clifton, where everything was laid out in neat blocks.

Over the Rio Grande Valley hung some clouds that had boiled up over the afternoon. To the west, one high cloud trailed rain that slanted backward and disappeared a little more than halfway to the ground. It reminded me of a jellyfish, floating over the valley, tendrils and tentacles floating behind, poised to grab and paralyze birds instead of fish.

I reached back and took the letter from my pocket. As I studied it, I was both terrified and curious to know what was inside. On one hand I thought I should destroy the letter, unopened. It probably said things that I shouldn't know—unguarded, naked things—drunken, private things. I hadn't watched my mother skinny-dipping and I was proud of that. Some words, I knew, should never be said. Some thoughts should always be secret. Some things should never be seen.

On the other hand, maybe it was just a regular letter, a letter. that she wrote and mailed before she decided to commit suicide. Or maybe it was a letter to tell me how much she loved me and not to blame myself for what she was about to do. There might be some things in the letter that I should know, things that might help me to live with what she had tried to do—or at least make it more understandable.

I went back and forth in my mind, not knowing what to do. Finally it grew too dark to read my name on the envelope. I put the unopened letter back into my pocket. Santa Fe was now a cloud of lights, a collection of constellations. I picked out shapes, making up patterns—a snake, a spoon, a loaf of bread—thinking how much the lights below looked like the stars reflected in my mother's swimming pool back in Iowa.

I imagined myself diving into them, scattering them in darkened waves. I felt like diving into the night and never coming up again.

When I heard Florence calling for me, I walked down the hill. I could feel the letter in my back pocket, but it could wait. I didn't need to decide right now. Maybe, in the next few days, I'd learn something that would help me decide.

My moods are like Iowa weather, not like New Mexico weather. When clouds arrive, they can stay for days, covering the sky from horizon to horizon. That's the way it was for me in the days following the letter.

The weather in Santa Fe was perfect and I resented it. It was as if the blue sky and the clear air were mocking my mood.

My mother's doctor called each day to let us know how she was doing. He told us that she was making progress, that she was out of her coma, that she was taking an antidepressant drug, that she was in therapy. I asked him to let me know when I could talk with her. Two Sundays had come and gone, and each Sunday I trudged up the hill at ten o'clock in the evening and talked to my mother through our star. Talking to her this way was better than nothing, but after the second time it felt childish and silly. It felt like playing a game instead of really communicating. My mother had always been big on games. I was tired of them. I longed to hear her voice and to tell her that I loved her—not through some star, but directly to her.

When the day finally arrived, when the doctor told

me I could call, I felt shy. What do you say to some-body who just tried to kill herself? Especially if she's your mother? "How's it going, going, gone?"

Florence and my father made it easier by excusing themselves to go on a walk. I dialed, got a hospital operator, told her the room number, and listened to the phone's phantom ring.

"Hello?"

It was my mother's voice, but I sensed that something was missing from it.

"Hello? Mom?"

"Chester!" Her voice suddenly took on life. It had been hollow and empty before. "How are you?"

That was to have been my first question to her, but she'd beat me to it. "Fine. How—how are you?"

There was a pause. I wondered if I should have asked. "Fine," she said. "Considering. I'm getting better every day."

"That's good." It was wonderful to hear her voice. "I've been thinking about you . . . a lot." I was scared to bring up the subject of her attempted suicide. But it was hard to dance around it like this.

"You've been thinking about me too much, proba-bly." Her voice was thinning, sounding more hollow. "Look, Chester"—she was rallying, sounding more en-ergetic—"let's not beat around the bush. I'm glad to be alive. Glad I didn't kill myself. I'm not very happy to be in this nuthouse, but I'm getting help."

"That's good." I was about to ask her about the let-ter when she continued, charging ahead. Some things just don't change.

"I want you to know how much I love you. Thinking about you has pulled me through some pretty black times lately. How's your father . . . and Florence?"

"Fine. They're doing fine." I tried to think of something more to say. "Dad's store is doing great and Florence's opening was a big success. She's going to California next week to see somebody about doing a commission."

"I'm glad to hear it." I don't know why it surprised me, but she actually sounded glad. "How are you feeling . . . about things?"

I didn't know quite what to say. "Fine."

She gave me a little more time to say something, and when I didn't she cleared her throat and said, "If I know you, Chester, you're brooding about things, moping around, and blaming yourself for—for everything that's happened. Am I right?"

Of course she was right. What was I supposed to say? So I said, "Yes."

"Well, I'm—I'm sorry and I—I don't want you to feel that way. It doesn't help. It wasn't your fault."

There was an awkward silence as I digested this. I didn't know what to say. It seemed as if she was still delicate, breakable, and I didn't want to say the wrong thing.

When she broke the silence, her voice was gentler, more in control. "Tell me about school. I don't even know what classes you're taking."

We talked for a long time—about everyday things that were suddenly important because they weren't important. My mother and I were still talking when Florence and my father came back from their walk. The more we talked, the easier it got. I wasn't feeling so shy anymore.

Finally my mother said, "Chester, the doctor just walked in and I can't keep him waiting. Would you call again in a couple of days?"

"Sure."

"I love you."

"I love you," I said, sounding like an echo.

" 'Bye."

" 'Bye." I didn't want to hang up.

And then I heard the dial tone.

FIFTEEN

▼▼▼▼▼▼▼▼▼▼▼

Snow came early, even for the high country in northern New Mexico. I had a hard time taking my eyes off
the mountains as my father, Florence, and I roasted
green chili in our backyard. The mountaintops were
sugar-white and looked as if they'd moved closer to us
during the night. And right below the snow stretched
a thick band of bright yellow aspen trees, with some
orange and a little red mixed in.

The smell of the roasting chili had just enough bite
to make the inside of my nose tingle when I breathed
in. I'd never smelled anything like it before, and I
couldn't think of how to describe it to my mother when
I talked with her next. Smoky? Spicy? Green?—as if
green had a smell.

We'd been roasting chili for two hours and we had a

long way to go. One gunnysack was beginning to shrink, turning into a lump on the driveway. The other sack stood straight—a giant burlap pillow on end, stuffed with waxy green chili pods about six inches long. We'd already added more charcoal to keep the fire hot. The pile of blistered and charred chili on the picnic table was growing, each chili steaming, its outside skin turning a milky color as it cooled enough to put into plastic bags for freezing.

"Watch out!" I yelled. One chili was puffing up, growing larger and larger, about to explode. I jabbed it with my long-handled fork and turned my head at the same time. I heard a messy pop and felt hot spots on the side of my neck and in my ear. I brushed off the chili-seed shrapnel and looked down at the grill. The chili had shrunk to its original size.

"That was close," Florence said, slipping her fork under a bright green bean and flipping it over. Its black crust was cracked, showing soft and steaming green flesh beneath.

"Chester! Chester!"

José ran up to us, panting, his eyes wide, a huge smile on his face.

"¡Milagro! ¡Milagro! It's a . . . miracle! Arturo . . . he's got . . . he's got the . . . Red Devil running!" He gulped for air. "I think . . . this time . . . this time it's for real!"

I could hardly believe it. "Can we take a ride?"

"That's . . . why I'm here . . . estúpido." José's breathing was becoming a little less labored.

"May I?" I asked, looking first at my father and then at Florence.

"Go on," my father said in a tired voice. "Just don't be too long. I'd like to get this done before midnight."

"Enjoy yourselves!" Florence sang as José and I raced down the driveway, turning left when we hit the street.

"I don't believe it!" I shouted. But I could hear the unmistakable rumble of a car coming from the direction of José's house.

"It needs . . . needs a new muffler," puffed José.

"But it's running!"

We rounded the house and there it sat, shaking and coughing in a cloud of blue smoke. Arturo sat behind the tiny chain steering wheel, grinning from ear to ear. I don't think I'd ever seen him so recklessly happy before.

José jumped up into the air and whooped, punching the sky with his fist.

We piled into the backseat through the passenger door. The sound of the engine echoed inside the car as if we were sitting in a beer can. Arturo draped his right arm over the front seat and turned enough to look at us. He was trying hard not to smile. "Want to go for a cruise?" he shouted above the noise.

"E-e-e-e! Yeah!" José shouted back, bouncing up and down on the seat. The car began to rock—front to back— like other low-riders I'd seen cruising around the Plaza.

"Hold on to your underwear!" Arturo shouted, jamming the car into gear. We lurched around the house and down the driveway, the car hiccupping and bucking. The car rode low to the ground—Arturo had "fixed" its suspension with a welding torch for now.

Turning the car with the tiny steering wheel must

have been difficult. Arturo's biceps bulged as he cranked and cranked to turn us onto the street. He let the steering wheel spin back into place as we started going straight. José and I leaned over the front seat and watched the road ahead. We crept down the street. The speedometer didn't work, so we didn't know how fast we were going. Five miles an hour was my guess. Arturo thought maybe ten.

"Now that I got the engine going," he shouted, "I'm going to really fix this thing up." He kept both hands on the steering wheel because even the smallest bump threw the Red Devil right or left.

The engine sounded as if it might die at any moment. And I could smell gas fumes coming through rust holes in the floor from the cracked muffler and tail pipe. But I didn't want to argue with Arturo. "Whatcha going to do?" I shouted in his ear.

His face took on a dreamy look, and José and I leaned over the front seat so we wouldn't miss anything he said. "Well, first I'm going to chrome and paint the engine . . . you know, the air manifold and the distributor cap . . . whatever I have enough money for. This engine will be so clean that you won't get your white gloves dirty."

"That costs a ton of money," José shouted. "How are you going to do that and go to college?" Arturo had just applied to the Technical Vocational Institute in Albuquerque.

Arturo shrugged. "I can take my time with the Red Devil. Hey, I know a guy who worked on his low-rider for ten years. And you should see it now. It's cher-ry!"

"And then what are you going to do . . . after the engine?" I was fascinated. Chrome engines! What next?

"Then I'll strip off all the paint . . . take it down to the metal . . . and then fix the rust cancer and paint it . . . oh, ten, twelve coats. You know, primer and then a special enamel . . . bright red . . . and then a couple coats of clear sealer on top of that. And I want flames . . . orange-red flames coming from the front wheel wells." He pulled a cigarette out of his shirt pocket and pressed it between his lips.

"And then, maybe, I can get Cousin Fernando to do an etching on the back window . . . of the Virgin or the Last Supper or Our Lady of Guadalupe or . . . something." I'd seen these before: beautiful designs, mostly religious, etched into low-rider windows, with borders of angels and vines.

A car was coming at us and Arturo raised his left arm in a salute. "Jimmy Tiny," he shouted to us, and then he slammed the car into neutral and gunned the engine. A terrifying rumble filled the Red Devil and I clamped my hands over my ears. The driver in the other car raised his hand in a salute and smiled as we cruised by. As soon as the engine was idling, Arturo threw it back into gear and we jolted down the road for a few seconds until it settled into a crawl.

I could see the pride in Arturo's face, in the way he held his jaw. It had always seemed silly to me, making such a big fuss over a car, but now I could see why Arturo did this. He'd made this piece of junk work and now he was going to make it beautiful.

"And then," Arturo continued, his voice slipping into

and out of the engine's roar, "I'm going to have Alicia reupholster the inside in crushed velvet . . . blue with a quilted design . . . even the visors."

We were stopped at a stop sign and Arturo turned to us. "Maybe, when I'm at school, you can work on the Red Devil . . . you know, help fix it up. And then when you get your driver's license you can maybe use it." There was no mistaking the pleasure he took in giving us the use of this car—even if it was all theoretical and far into the future.

"No-o-o-o!" José couldn't believe his ears.

"Yes!" Arturo shouted happily, creeping across the intersection. "But if you mess up . . . if your grades aren't good . . . if you drink in this car and drive . . . then I take away the keys."

José fell back into the backseat, overwhelmed by his brother's generosity.

"That means you too, Chester." Arturo grinned at me. I smiled back, remembering all the times I'd seen his rear end sticking up as he leaned into the engine of the Red Devil, trying to get something to work.

My ears tingled from our ride as José walked with me to my house. We'd cruised for an hour or so, stopping once to add more oil to the engine—not a good sign—and stopping once more to let some friends of Arturo's admire the engine and ooh and aah over the Red Devil's promise as he described what he was going to do.

There was a question I wanted to ask José, and I decided that this was as good a time as any.

"Hey, José. Would you like to go back with me to

Iowa for Thanksgiving . . . when I visit my mom?" I wanted José to come with me for a lot of reasons—my mother would be on her best behavior if I had a guest—I wanted to share Clifton with José so that he could see where I grew up—having José with me would be like bringing to Iowa some of the happiness and strength I'd found in Santa Fe.

But there was also a part of me that would be relieved if he said no. What if my mother had been trying to sound better on the phone than she really was? What if José thought Clifton was a drab, boring little town?

"Hey!" He beamed. "Hey, I'd love to go to Ohio with you. E-e-e-e! Maybe we can see some elephant eyes." And then he pretended to be serious. "Or do those elephants fly south for the winter?"

My hair still smelled of smoke and green chili as I pulled the covers to my chin. The window was partway open and I wondered if Tuxedo Cat would sneak inside while I slept and curl up at my feet, as he had last night—it was getting cold at night now. There would be no moon and the night would be dark. Even so I was keeping my glasses on until the very last moment—maybe it's my imagination, but lately I seem to think more clearly with my glasses on, even in the dark. I thought of the stars glimmering above me. And then I thought about the drawing that hung across the room that I could not see in the dark. José had given it to me yesterday—a drawing of Tuxedo Cat curled up in his favorite chair in Florence's studio.

I also thought about that letter from my mother that was still unopened and hidden under the mattress as far as my arm could reach.

My mother and I had talked a lot over the past few weeks. But one thing we didn't talk about was the letter. I was afraid to mention it, and she never brought it up. I don't know if that was because she didn't remember writing it or because she wasn't feeling well enough to deal with it or because it wasn't all that important compared with all the other things she was dealing with. I still went back and forth, wondering if I should throw it out or not. I always ended up undecided, which meant keeping it and not opening it.

But tonight, after the wonderful day I'd just had, I felt brave enough to open the letter and read it. If I did, I wouldn't have to worry about opening it up anymore.

I rolled over onto my stomach, leaned over the edge of the bed, and reached under the mattress as far as my arm would go. I groped for a couple of seconds before I felt the edge of the envelope. Locking my fingers, I pulled it out. Slipping out of bed, I walked quietly to my desk, felt for the lamp switch, and flicked it on.

My hand shook slightly. I stared at my name on the envelope and pressed my lips together. Knowing that if I didn't open it quickly I would chicken out, I peeled back a corner of the flap, stuck my finger in, and slit the side. I yanked out the letter: three sheets of stationery, sloppily folded.

My heart was beating in my throat as I unfolded it. I lifted it closer to my face so that I could read my mother's kinked handwriting.

Dearest Chester,

I long to be lying on my pillow of clouds, to sleep forever, to dream only good dreams. I keep remembering a poem of yours—one about a bird. Remember it? Of course you do. It's the one that goes—

> *The window looked like*
> *Sky reflected in*
> *Heaven is swooping*
> *Soaring up to*
> *Clouds that slide, skidding on*
> *Glass the bird saw floating*
> *Plunged down with a*
> *Snap to . . .*
> *Death in my hand*
> *I hold a bird with whiskers*
> *By its beak point*
> *Delicately their wings*
> *Fold back when dead.*

I've thought about that a lot, Chester. It's such a lovely poem—confused and disturbing and melancholy. Fractured. And shattering. I'm headed for the window, Chester. The clouds look so wonderful. I pray that—

I closed my eyes against what I was reading, knowing that what I'd just read told me everything I needed to know. And I was shocked, shocked to see my words in her handwriting on the page. I didn't like having my words thrown back in my face, especially because my mother was using them to explain what she'd done—or tried to do. She really had meant to kill herself. I think I'd known it all along.

How could she do that?—use my words that way! Words are dangerous things when they're used the wrong way, when they're twisted around to mean something terrible. My mother had made my own words dangerous. She'd aimed them back at me, aimed them right between my eyes, and they hurt enough to make me cry.

At last I left the letter on my desk, turned out the desk lamp, and crawled into bed, feeling more like a bug than a person. And like a bug I flipped over onto my back and felt helpless.

As I looked up at where the ceiling was supposed to be, I could almost hear my mother's voice saying those words. "I long to be lying on my pillow of clouds." How could she turn such a beautiful image into something so awful? And then I heard her voice again, saying, "I pray that—" I cut her off again.

I could finish her letter for her now—any way I wanted. And I could change the ending, make it happy. "I pray that—"

What is a prayer, anyway? I was beginning to change my opinion of them. I used to think praying was stupid. Prayers always seemed to be ways of expressing hope—what you hope people think of you—what you hope you can be—what you hope will happen—what you hope the world will be like. And prayers didn't need to be spoken in the dark to a dial tone. They didn't need to be prayed only to God. They could be prayed to oneself. And prayers didn't need to be only words. They could be expressed in other ways. José's drawings were his prayer. Arturo's low-rider was his prayer. Florence's paintings were her prayer. My father's novel was his prayer. My poetry was my prayer.

What was my mother's prayer? Maybe that was what was wrong with her: She needed a prayer. We all need prayers.

"I pray that"—and then I finished the sentence for her—"we grow to love ourselves and that our lives become our prayers."

Closing my eyes I imagined myself lying on a pillow of clouds, comfortable and safe and soft, sinking just so far.

I heard the soft thump of a cat landing on my bedroom floor and waited for the weight of Tuxedo Cat as he jumped up onto my bed.

I wasn't disappointed.

CPSIA information can be obtained
at www.ICGtesting.com
Printed in the USA
FSOW02n0939170816
23887FS

9 780595 097708